The Love Letters of
Lydia Swangarden

Rocco Scibetta

ISBN 978-1-954345-91-1 (paperback)
ISBN 978-1-954345-93-5 (digital)

Rushmore Press LLC
1 800 460 9188
www.rushmorepress.com

Printed in the United States of America

Wednesday, 1:30 PM
Notes

The designer of infants in all its ancient wisdom has done an extraordinary thing. He or she has kept beauty encapsulated to the eye of the beholder. If the designer had not done so, an unchecked reaction of cause and effect would send people diving out of windows and cause strong men to weep.

I understand that girls just want to have fun and that my mid-life crisis is an aging teenage illness best left to the care of bartenders and psychologists, but the story I am about to recall brought me surprise and shock with each event that unfolded. But first, I must tell you about Lydia—my heart, my muse, and in a reverse way, myself. We were nothing alike, but how I wish I could have been like her.

Her life was a grand adventure. The most extraordinary things just seemed to happen with her.

She was grandiose.

One never knew what was to lie beyond each bend, twist, or fork in the road. Chance meetings and karma—not to mention surreal opportunity—just seemed to happen with her. She never worried what tomorrow might bring; she just attracted happenings.

I cannot say that I have never seen her unhappy or despondent in any way during our short time together. Fate had gifted her lavishly. She was pretty and well to do, if not rich altogether. No one knew for sure of the Swangarden's net worth, but whatever it was—it kept Lydia on the trust fund path for all her years. She was a child of Jupiter. It was in her nature to dream the impossible dream.

We were so unlike.

I would huddle safety at every turn; I need not say that if the evolution of civilization were up to me, things would get done slowly, if not by accident; or not at all.

Art? I have only a superficial depth for it, although I did, at one time, aspire to become a journalist—if that fits into the narrow constraints of what we define art as nowadays. The quest for what makes literature important always confounded me. Lydia, on the other hand, had no use for art whatsoever but understood it completely. Devouring it like medication, absorbing it as one might absorb an aspirin for a headache. The brilliance of high art never unsteadied her; she quickly became it, as though it were the latest fashion or trend. The flow and tide of style and fancy footwork that brought about contemporary exaltation rest like laurel leaves on her head. She saw the wisdom in comic strips and could envision Nefertiti in bell-bottom pants and a two-dollar hat. She grabbed at once the commercialism of a big America. A Faberge egg is something that would never interest her. She would scoff, "There should be more Faberge chickens." A search for greener pastures always pursues.

I was not altogether truthful in telling you about the cremation. Yes, it was raining, and yes, I did stand outside and watch the smoke puff the final memory I will have of L. However, there was more.

The one detail I could not bring myself to recap for fear that the horror of it might lead me into the unpleasant description of distaste and, above all, dishonor to Lydia on her final resting day was this: I had been sneaking around the grounds of the cremation facility trying to find the main office; I had arrived much earlier than I had originally said. Why I would lie about a small insignificant detail such as that is in itself a tell. Am I refraining from the truth? Why? I don't know myself to honestly answer. The answer might be what keeps me awake at night; the disease that has stunted my ambition in journalism has eventually led me here some thirty odd years later to this backlog of memory and depression—the lot and grounds of this crematorium.

I hoped to find someone in-charge lurking around, a dupe I might speak with that could allow me a private viewing; some way I could see L without associating with the gathering of whoever might be in those hideous pews. (I don't want to go inside; I did not go inside.)

Of course, to do it the conventional way and go directly to the office and speak with the director of cremation services would make me too nervous. I would stutter and shake and appear odd. They would ask too many questions; to all of which my answers would sound quirky and perverted.

I mean, how am I to explain that I need to see a tattoo on the deceased? Or request a photo of it?

It was a love letter I was informed of—a love letter or a collection of sentences—from shoulder to spine written in the arcane script.

I have only heard about it but have never seen it for it was well after our intimate time together; why now, if this was the case, should I be informed of it? The fact that it might have been written to or about me was always the mystery. It can do me no good; only disturb me.

Her back was huge, after all; what a sizable writing surface! It was no wonder that she was not to be buried at a normal cemetery. Not being a religious man myself, I have some knowledge of religions that prohibit it—the unholy deprivation of the flesh and all that. Not to mention her brand of religion was never conventional by any stretch and never carried out to any full conviction.

No, Lydia was a Jupiter child; she obeyed the stars in the sky and was comfortable with their orbit. We never discussed religion. I am not sure if she was an atheist or not, being that she was seventeen when we first met. I doubt if any firm religious conviction could have formulated in her soul. That being said, allow me to finish my thought without getting too ahead of myself.

I believe, partly because of the foul weather and partly because of the deadline scheduling demands, all doors were locked except for one. As fate would have it, I noticed a small hunched-over figure entering a shanty garage off and away from the main facility that appeared to be a sort of refuse area. Leaping over some puddles, I then made my way to a window that was just about my height. I pulled over a cinder block that elevated me just high enough so that I can look in. It was here that my view of life and death and the disposal of our earthly shackles brought me to the realization that we are but spokespersons for a carnival; representatives for a traveling show we call existence and demise.

The figure was seated at a small desk, eating what appeared to be a canned fish product. I knocked on the window, jolting him with surprise. With nowhere to go, he confronted me with hand gestures, directing me to go around to the front entrance and shooing me away. Talking loudly over the pounding rain, I pleaded with him to come to the door and speak with me, which he was hesitant to do. Most likely thinking I was a distressed mourner unable to find my way into the crematorium, he nervously motioned me to come to the door, and he let me in. It was not long before I realized that this was the man who brought the box containing L's remains to the dumpster; he was in charge of maintaining the grounds work and prepping the manual needs for the cremation service. Over his shoulder, behind a curtain, I noticed the edges of the gurney.

This was it, I thought to myself, *Lydia*. My heart leaped into my throat. My face betrayed me to the crypt keeper, and my speech sped up and began to sound nervous—like a lunatic. I must stay calm and not get excited. Talk persuasively about my intention.

"Sir," I said. "Thank you for your time. I know that you are very busy. There is something I must bring to your attention—a slight overlook, perhaps; understandable with all your other responsibilities and such miserable weather—but there is a remains carton by the parking lot. I thought you might want to know in the event some of the visitors see. It could be uncomfortable for them as it was for myself…"

"Oh dear," he declared, shaking a piece of sardine loose from his lower lip. "I am deeply sorry, sir. Thank you so much for your discreetness in coming to me first; I will get it immediately."

"I will assist you. With the rain and all, it could be a mess for you; I don't mind. I understand your dilemma, and I do thank you—on behalf of the Swangardens—for showing due diligence in this matter."

"Of course," the shaky little man responded.

He pulled some rain gear from a hook, and we made our way past the lawn and the parking area to the refuse area where the sizable carton was drooping in the rain. Folding it into a manageable structure, we proceeded to hoist it into a ready dumpster. Hurrying back, I followed the crypt keeper to his shanty workspace. He was slightly perturbed that I followed him back. I presume he was hoping that, having completed my mission, I would go back to the chapel or my car.

There was something odd with the man, a nervousness he kept under wraps. He spoke in riddles as if to feel me out; I felt he did not trust I was truthful in my intent. Little messages would roll out from his fishy breath as he mumbled over his shoulder.

"Are you with someone? You're the second one..." he blurted out, quickly correcting himself before canceling his words. He had mousey little eyes that kept shifting to a flat box leaning by his desk. It was taped securely with no markings. Then, he would glance at me as if waiting for a password or something—slick and coveting as he was, his subtle demeanor was no match for my critical paranoia. I picked up on him immediately. I knew this creepy little man had something to hide.

I suspected I should leave; he was making me feel out of place. There was skullduggery between this crypt keeper and that box, and I am in between it.

He began to talk in riddles about people in question, The Swangardens, and a mysterious man. I quickly surmised there was a secret he was hiding behind. I couldn't make out if he was nuts or just being friendly when he brought up a mutual interest (a certain tattoo); it was then that I knew what he had on his mind. He kept looking at the aforementioned box and looked back at me. He said there was something he had to mail. I believe he thought I was someone else. Another character in this rogue's gallery... perhaps the mysterious man he referred to at the cremation; the svelte older chap escorting the young lady who was pushing old man Swangarden up the handicap ramp.

I don't mind telling you, Vlad; the whole experience was, to say the least, nauseating. The slight trace of sardines and vinegar marinade that exuded from the crypt keeper was enough for me to toss my cookie, as they say; that being said, not eating a decent meal over the last few days just resulted in some harmless stomach gurgling and chest pain. Once he deduced that I was not the person he presumed me to be, I am sure the crypt keeper had wanted me to go away at that point, to bid him goodbye and go about my business; but I did not. I had to pursue my true purpose—to see Lydia's love letters (or letter) tattooed across her back. But had I have known of the package waiting for me...

> Oh, Lydia! Oh, Lydia! Say, have you met Lydia?
> Oh! Lydia, the tattooed lady
> She has eyes that folks adore so
> And a torso even more so
> Lydia, oh! Lydia, that "Encyclopedia"
> Oh! Lydia, the Queen of Tattoo
> On her back is the Battle of Waterloo
> Beside it the Wreck of the Hesperus too
> And proudly above the waves
> The Red, White, and Blue
> You can learn a lot from, Lydia

One week later

A small cluster of neighborhood moms meets in front of the brownstone steps every morning, just two floors below my window, to kibitz and gossip. It is a common ritual for the girls to pull their carriages into designated squatter spots, placing themselves on the stoop and waiting for the chain reaction of wailing to begin. *Stoop* the neighborhood colloquialism for front steps.; now, that word can betray me. Not unlike parlor or candy stores, those have long been renamed living rooms and convenience centers. Change happens.

It is self-revealing, how I was attracted to this apartment. There was nothing in its fundamental location or urban makeup that stirred any interest in me. I am alone and single a blue-collar working stiff. I have no particular fondness for children or pets or domestic life (not anymore). I have built an oasis of books and paintings, and I am quite self-medicated with the kind of music I am comfortable with.

I feel strange—a little worse than usual. The dampness from the humidly below, rising off the pavement and pulling from the street was making me lethargic. It is a little better now. The mess that is gray cotton balls forming in my head is thick with weevils.

The calendar taped to the wall was still highlighted. October 5th, on the day of our Lord, Wednesday—I should have been preparing to march down to the local mental health clinic to describe my feelings of high anxiety and melancholia until I was notified by mail that the mental health clinic would not see me anymore.

Not because my feelings of paranoia and depression have suddenly gone away, leaving me happy and robust and no longer in need of their service, but because I missed two appointments in a row.

I feel so loved.

I know some could have benefited from your magic, had I informed you sooner of my cancelation.

I understand it is not personal. It is a business.

Of course, how paranoid, schizophrenic, and depressed of me not to know the difference between personal and business.

I presume they suspect me of not being grateful for their magic— getting lax, maybe, taking the meds for granted, and jamming up the process. They could have used valuable time and resources on real people, along with the state check that compensates them per patient visit.

Let me go instead to Assumption Hall and visit my good friend and keeper of the faith, Brother Vlad. I will pack a thermos of coffee and some strong drink in the form of cognac to open the mind's eye. We are only human, you know.

Father Vlad, the inhaler—so-called for his slack jaw and hanging lower lip—is a good man. Despite his tendency to mouth breath, no other signs of low intelligence are visible in him.

I do not want to bore anyone over there in the mental health building with my excuses—not the magician or the usher, not even the ticket agent that takes my card. Therefore, I will renegotiate my appointment scheduling to their convenience. That being said, I still feel like shit.

On my kitchen table, there is half a cup of coffee, two cigar butts crushed in an ashtray, an open notebook, a pen, and some empty packages from last night's dinner; but the item of interest that concerned me the most is a box from FedEx that I have not yet opened.

It came addressed to Wellington Montgomery 14-courtyard place. (That would be me.) It is only half a mystery; however, I have some clue as to its contents from a letter that came two days ago from attorneys Wigdor, Sherman, and Strauss. They are estate lawyers retained no doubt to find me and deliver this cryptic prize to my doorstep; bounty hunters for the Grim Reaper. The letter stated that *upon the death of Lydia Collette Swangarden, the contents contained therein consisting of one framed artifact and a scrapbook journal be delivered to the person bearing the name above*—bingo!

To whom it may concern: I talk to myself. This is a fact. I have no real friends; that being said, I will address my modest audience of imaginary guests—you little hobgoblins of pranks and circumstances that dance on the head of a pin celebrating each travesty that befalls me. It won't be long for me now; I choked out twice at the end of a rope but did not dare to finish the execution. I am growing more comfortable with the idea of death every day, and soon I will succeed. You see I am a coward in death even more so than I am in life, which might explain why Lydia was such a life driving force in me. Much of the sickness that is in me comes from the aggression of Lydia's modern life. I believe so, anyway. But beauty heals me; Lydia healed me. She could project from another place. I believe that.

At times I thought I saw the other in her—and still do, or did; healing comes when I get into a supernatural space where I can enjoy the beauty. She is dead now; did I mention that?

When most people look at something beautiful, it makes them happy. What I experienced from Lydia was not like that. It was the dark thing that was in her that was beautiful.

In human relationships, the burgeoning of personal love must be amongst living things. This was not living. It was an emotion that aroused sickness in me. I have not noticed this in others—only in myself and, sometimes, with Lydia when she was reflecting. I labeled the anxiety I was experiencing *reflecting* because, like I said, it came from another place inside her—not her body, not her mind, but an inner sanctum between soul and spirit; the dark place I cannot understand. You see, everything we choose is a reflection of our personalities. Lydia sometimes said her personality was a mirror; that darkness in her that sometimes revealed itself was a living looking glass of connection and communication. Of course, I was not able to judge because they have chosen a different way for me—*they* being Lydia and the other—an invisible forbearing that crippled me for years to come. Do not get me wrong; it was not always such. In between the darkness and light, there was normality.

Let me begin by telling a little bit about myself.

My humble beginnings are not so much different than that of the Dickens character Pip, in that we share the same brevity in namesake, and both of us (Pip and I) fell sucker to a pretty face.

My mother's maiden name being Montchevalier and my father's sir name being Montgomery—it was all my infant tongue could come to pronounce was Monte. It was soon thereafter; I was to be called Monte. And Monte I was known as all the days of my life.

The Christian name notarized and documented in the year of our Lord, February 12, 1967; on my baptismal papers is Wellington Gunner Montgomery a nomenclature I had very little use for; I am Monte. The only deviation in name use occurred during that short summer when, for a precious time, the hypocorism of "Bubs" was bestowed upon me—a name granted by Miss Lydia Swangarden in memory of Miss Swangarden's deceased cat "Bubbsy," short for Beelzebub. She called me Bubs because I was such a pussycat.

Of all of the culture-changing events that formed my life the year of my birth—thereby affecting the years after—only two seemed to have a direct impact on my outcome as a functioning adult: the summer of love and the year of the fire goat. This is the sign for good or bad that hung over me.

Those born between February 9, 1967, and January 29, 1968, belong to the Chinese zodiac sign of the Fire Goat. Goat people are elegant, charming, generous, wise, and gentle. They are also pessimists, hesitant, and over-anxious worriers. Uncertainty causes the people of the Goat sign to seek guidance from others while their timidity prevents them from becoming great leaders. They are deeply religious and highly talented in the fields of art and music. Goat people should be good in the professions of gardening, acting, artistry, entertainment, music, or photography.

However, those born during the winter of the year of the summer of love—not so much so; their parents were most likely indulging in the promiscuity of campus life as mine were two dopey hippies.

I was born a free spirit child of the universe—a Goat child being led through the field by hippie sheepherders in the age of Aquarius; so much for religion.

A scrapbook aye—that is what they are calling it for lack of a better name—a curious little item of nostalgia to be held in my hand once again. Beeswax, quaint—I am becoming a wheelbarrow of antiquated terms and endearments these days.

Before I open this box, let me check my hoarder's den for that cassette player under that heap of once-cool stuff. I might want to play some old music cassettes to welcome the ghosts. Perhaps Raspberries' "Go All the Way" or some Badfinger songs. I am sure I have top 40 icons and one-hit wonders around here somewhere, packed away in the same carton the Rolodex is in—amazing that I still have these items; things best brought to antique stores.

I have to remind myself this is the digital age now. How interwoven my generation was to those sights and sounds; how psychologically tattooed—permanently scarred.

Somewhere in my future, I must have gotten lost. The future accelerates so quickly; only the past lingers like a headache, looking out from a car window at eighty miles per hour.

I still have those addresses; over thirty years now, I can still remember my home phone number at my parents' house: 683-5721. Ha, no special dialing required before the area code in those days; didn't need it. We had not yet reached the phone number crisis that caused us to make up new number combinations… folks are long gone.

I get dizzy in old cellars and cluttered closets sometimes. When the last of my parents died a few moments ago—I meant to say summers ago—I rummaged through an old suitcase that was up in the attic for close to a century. I was tossing things out, making space. Good feng shui; less clutter clears the mind—good for your health and karma. Amidst some old shirts and souvenir, there was a seashell with hypnotic iridescent rainbow inlays. It was affixed to a plaster base, pink coral sprouting up from its center, with a plastic pink flamingo glued into varnished sand. A small light fixture was attached behind the shell adding a chintzy glow when lit; "Greetings from Florida," was hand-painted across the base. I remember this; it was a keepsake of my parents. It was kept on a shelf in my parents' bedroom. I sometimes played with it as a child, fascinated by the combination of different objects.

The cheap texture and intactness of the object stirred fresh nostalgia in me—one ghostly memory I had suppressed for a very long time. I stopped everything I was doing to find an outlet to plug it in and turn it on… It worked. The worker who had glued its parts together at a factory somewhere in Florida is probably long dead. I think of who it might have been—maybe a housewife trying to earn a few bucks gluing things together in a hundred-degree room so tourist chumps could buy these crummy nightlights; as they think back on their once-in-a-lifetime vacation, that was most likely more trouble than it was worth in those days.

Well, looky here! A tarnished pen—bronze, metallic, and encrypted with an automobile ad. It reads in faded black ink, "Bowens used cars." If you tilted it slowly, the center would slide back behind the plastic tubing, revealing a miniature statuette of a lovely beach babe from the 1950s. No detail; she might be naked. Hot stuff; getting some insight into my old man's thoughts on subtle ad porn through the things he collected. Most ads of that sort were solely for the entertainment of men in those days. The night light was probably Mom's; the kinky pens and little folding pen knives were Dad's. The compartments of the mind were as carefully segregated as gender roles.

I can't think of what Lydia collected all these years… and why she had to have it sent to me.

Shit! If one thing falls on me in here. I am not opening that box. I'm gonna fling it on top of this mountain of I-do-not-know-what… Ah, up top left-hand corner, I see the wedge of it. Two letters LAU…

that is Lauren, all right. That is the one; stuff she left behind. It's in there with her astrology book, lava lamps, and weird hippie shit—pretty sure.

Bring it down slowly; don't slip. If I break my fucking hip in here, I am going to be really pissed.

There is a firm,_foothold between these two crates—right footholds... Hold on to that coat rod; strong galvanized pipe won't bend under pressure. Stretch just a little more... fingertip tear in a carton... Got it! Come on, slide. Slide—easy does it—two inches more and it's free. *Ugh*, got it down. Whew!

On second thought, maybe there was an unconscious attraction I had for this apartment after all.

The house that I was raised in as a child was a simple one-family structure—cookie-cutter beige and brown planted firmly in the middle of the block.

A few houses down from mine and across the street, where the sidewalk came to a dead-end, stood the Swangarden monstrosity; the compound, as I called it. The Swangarden place took up about three lots. It was a mansion by our standards and loomed over our tiny houses with grotesque obscenity and obscure dimensions.

I lived there at 78 Cottage Street with my mom, my dad, and my sister until the illness and death of both parents. And the eventual marriage of my sister Beth pushed my hand into matrimony of my own.

I married Lauren after six tedious years of courtship, thereby relinquishing my journalism career and all other hopes and dreams into the abyss to play house for five more years until the bough finally broke.

I aspired to become a family man at this time.

You believe it—little starter home, picket fence, a postage-stamp patch of lawn, all that happy horse shit; a regular Joe, no kids though, much to my advantage; easy divorce in and out. She went her way, and I went mine with just the house in tow. We divided up the difference and parted as friends. I never saw her again. Lauren was a stickler to keep her figure. She found a guy right away.

I thought it was romantic to gloom over it for a while, like lovers often do, but quickly realized she was living in L.A. with a jewelry salesman and didn't give a flying fuck through a donut hole if I was alive or dead. So, I moved on.

That was Lauren; this is Lydia—I could never get them confused. I have a parcel post package before me from the ghost trustees at Wigdor, Sherman, and Strauss.

Hunting around in this decaying old shit brings out the kid in me. Constructive collection for folks that do that kind of thing is good I suppose; to love something enough to want to save it, somewhat (moved by its magic)—art or whatever—is healthy sometimes. Collecting objects associated with a time or place is a healthy fantasy that can bring you back to a time and place, even if that time and place were never healthy for you. That being said, perhaps clinging to the past through fairytale objects is not so healthy after all. Still and all, there are things I hold on to. Lydia knows this about me. Hence, the package, a real sweetheart.

The era I was born into was a crossover time. Cultures were overlapping, and there was a group identity crisis that brought on a cultural upheaval and left my generation confused for years. There were wars and rumors of wars that turned out to be bloodletting skirmishes more than anything else. There was a new mindset in the air; the new generation wanted to make love, not war. Our parents were getting old. I suppose coming of age and realizing mortality inflicted a painful awareness of the mistakes from the past. There were obvious holes in the foundation that was supporting many. Atlas was shrugging and crowds of young people were diving off the edge of the world in desperation.

There were flags people waved espousing symbols of peace and change. Everyone chanted for freedom from something. It took years and much disheartening revelation to realize their idols had clay feet. No one can promise you anything if you are not able to accept the delivery. There was no gold and nothing substantial to carry the future. Just piles of bell-bottom pants and old books about revolution gathering dust at the redemption army store.

However, what I have here are stacks of shit. They mean nothing to the collective world—only to me and I am fading.

Of all my adolescent memories, there is one that stands out that seems to haunt me more than the rest—at least for a few seconds every day. I dedicate time and memory to that perverse image of Lydia Swangarden playing basketball at the courts. The courts were a small city park with hoops and swings; a metal gazebo with benches, gated and institutionalized. It was overstated with dedication plaques and trees from formidable politicians and pillars of the community. The idea was to provide an outlet for the urban youth so they would not smoke pot or sniff glue and go crazy with the draft being unpopular, and the culture going to hell. The future generation needed something to do to keep their mind off the forthcoming adult dismay.

Lydia, was five-foot-nine inches tall and all of seventeen when I first laid eyes on her. Innocent as it was, I thought nothing of it. She was a new girl in the neighborhood; I was twenty-seven and working in a factory that made brass nipples for the pipe.

Me sprouting to only five-foot-six and not very athletic myself, I can tell you I was no one's choice for the center on the neighborhood basketball teams when they were choosing sides. But Lydia was. She was incredibly gifted in athletics: tall and strong, focused, and strategically smart with game plans.

In the evenings, sometimes, I would sit on the steps in front of the house and watch her play ball. No one could help but notice how confident she was competing with the boys. One Saturday afternoon, she was alone at the basketball courts shooting hoops. She became aware of me watching her from the stoop. She came over, and we became friends. Sometimes, we would play one-on=one basketball; she would cover me so closely, her breasts always colliding with my shoulder and forearm. She was no dainty flower at five-nine in gym shorts and sports tee; sweating only added to her earthy appeal.

At this point the neighbors took no real interest in our intentions; it was when she began to visit me on my front steps giggling and flirting that rumors started to bubble. Maybe it was the way she sat that disturbed the den mothers—knees always up or slightly parted. "Sit, ladies, like you are squeezing a quarter between your knees." Not Lydia.

Well, as I was saying, I awoke this morning in my new apartment overlooking the Truman schoolyard. Glancing out my window over the young mothers assembled outside, nothing was unusual.

I felt slightly nervous in my stomach about this package—slight anxiety. All this to do about nothing; what did I know about Lydia anyway? A few lively summers in a young man's life; precious as they were… Life in the nineties; everyone was carrying on. There were huge illusions about power and prestige.

From the dim view of my simple and humdrum life, the perspective changed daily. The impetuous mysteries were bold and beautiful. You could notice it all around you, but you could not gather any real knowledge from it. The view from my window became like a phony piece of artwork that doesn't truly exist in nature; the way self-delusion doesn't exist naturally. First, you must be bullshitted some way. Then, the bullshit must be maintained and convincing, or its life is short-lived. At times, it became a frenzy of fast-talkers and world-weary traveling salesmen showing up in your neighborhood with foreign cars and bags of take-out food order—beggars no more.

Some have dedicated whole life practices to sustain the illusion that they are somebody; the ego had to be maintained, like the tune-up on a Ferrari.

Everyone stampeded toward the steps of Babylon except me and my Lydia.

I suppose the distinguishing marks of sin are determined by how long they go on in memory; otherwise, it is… what? I have paid for my sins doubly, triply maybe, throughout the course of my life. Lydia had the memory of a honeybee going from one flower to another, according to the needs of her youthful passions. Is it the moon's fault people stop and stare at it in dreaming, casting wishes upon it—that old pocked face; emblem of nursery rhymes. No wish ever came true on the moon's account, I can tell you that. Some end their lives in the light of it; some come close, while others just come to their senses. These folks are not moon cursors or worshippers, I can tell you that; are they not all equal in their despair when they are disappointed by broken promises or unanswered prayers? I have not gotten away with anything. Instead, I gained this box.

My anxiety is bad today. I am sure if I am talking to myself. I can feel the mumbling through the vibration on my lips. I fear the mirror. I dread that one day I will look into it and it will be someone else looking back at me. Not the devil, and not the Lord, but an untamed spirit that has been watching Lydia and me all this time. It knows our secrets.

After all these years, Lydia wants me to have something. This box of horror and I cannot refuse her because she is dead. Oh, she is gone. The soft tufted ginger hair, those pale blue eyes. Oh, sweet Jesus, she is coming in here...I knew it would not be a good idea to go into my garage but she wanted to see it. See what I do here: Fix things; change the oil in my car. Kiss her passionately... I had to push her away when she would not stop-Yeah, oh yeah... the little vixen was full of tricks "I won't stay long, I know what they are saying," she would say.

Here, wait... Let me pluck some flowers from Zampella's yard, and throw them at your pine box. My absent darling, here, have more; cover it nicely. Nice, you sweat lip... your insatiable foul body of gas and bubbles going up in smoke, leaving a great smoldering pile grayer than cigar ash.

I am glad you did not send me your urn; I would have desecrated it with the tears that I shed now for this ugly box before me... letters and notes with your name, you witch. A journal from which I could read your thoughts from the grave. Ouch, do you hear me now piercing my flesh on Zampella's crummy thorn bushes? How she yelled at me when I cut some roses from her garden to surprise you with that magical afternoon. Shut up, Zampella! I will take as many of your prize roses as I want. It is Lydia who needs them now... not your garden, not the earth... only Lydia.

> Oh, Lydia! Oh, Lydia! Say, have you met Lydia?
> Oh! Lydia, the champion of them all
> She once swept an Admiral clear off his feet
> The ships on her hips made his heart skip a beat
> And now the old boy is in command of the fleet
> George Fenton. Groucho Marx?

Come out on the dance floor where I can see you. Tell some jokes; there is some sponge cake on your mustache. Vaudeville is over.

Like I said, at seventeen she was budding and spry and only five foot nine when our secret romance had begun. I was almost thirty.

When Lydia was twenty-one and could legally drink—that was the year I believe she stopped growing, and we had stopped seeing each other. I thought she peaked at six foot four-and one-half inches tall. I was surprised she continued growing for many more years.

In heels, she was the Eiffel tower.

The term summer of love, the year of my birth, has long since become a buzzword for enthusiasts of the era I was born into; books and volumes of literature were written about it. The idealities and happenings still project a kind of mystery tour. Fantasy sorcerers that spoke a secret language using symbols and catchphrases continue to hypnotize the public with enchiridia about alternate lifestyles. The Beach Boys brought brightness and melancholia… Like the last line written to a summer love in the letter you were certain would endear her closer to you forever—the beautiful misery of wanting something you could never have. The morbid peace of that moment when you were sure you would never see them again; what phonies we were in those days. *La douleur exquise.* The endless summer.

September brought everyone back to their hometowns, leaving vinyl sounds in cheap cardboard covers, committing to the senses long after the heart has fogged; psychedelic advertising could bring you its own synthesized version of your memory. Whatever you needed to hear was there in your teenage heart—there was a song for it; whatever you needed to see, there was an image.

I was born into a continuum. Rock stars and zealots and wizards of all types—I have only heard the stories. I came into my own in the seventies. My own time was quite dull in comparison. It is difficult walking in the shadow of a prior epoch, like living with a twin sibling you will never know. Lydia made that reference more than once. She spoke sometimes as if she was speaking for two; like a ghost at the parade. Now that I think of it, I never felt alone with her. More than a quarter of a century later for me, there was only Lydia—the embodiment of all things gone by… and another, watching.

A reincarnation of the year I was born—my twin soul. She was earth mother, child of the universe. The Jupiter child.

I learned everything a young man needs to know about women's underwear from Lydia.

I would watch her from my back window. She would hang her delicate undies on the line early in the morning after the neighborhood blue-collar guys went off to work. I am sure she did it for my benefit. She knew I was there. We had a code. I pulled up my shade, and she knew I was watching.

The Swangardens had an electrical clothes dryer, no doubt about that; ole lady Barngarten always up on the newest appliances. Sometimes ole Lady Barngarten would sun herself on the patio deck. Patio… does anyone say patio anymore? God, I am a relic. She was *something else*, the old lady. I call her the "old lady," but she was closer to my age than Lydia was. Hot lookin' older babe. Two-piece bikini—I always imagined the ole lady in her underwear. Was that cheating on Lydia?

> Some are satin some are silk,
> Some are cotton white as milk.

One of her little poems when she was being silly, especially when she suspected me of fantasying about her stepmother.

My first and most fond memory was her high school graduation—Lydia in her post-mod dress so artsy and fashionable. No bra, of course; the freedom statement of the wealthy, decadent upper-middle-class.

No one knew the ages exactly. When she was sixteen or seventeen, or somewhere around it—timeframes are a little fuzzy to me now, for this all taking place close to a half-century ago—Lydia Barngarten mesmerized me. She was running back and forth from the house to the car; always scatter-brained, always frantic. They were celebrating something. The Swangardens were always celebrating something.

Her father, Herbert Swangarden, was a carpet distributor to major hotel chains across the country. I thought nothing of it at the time. The man's occupation was invisible to me. In fact, how I came to learn anything about him was as bizarre and convoluted as any part of this tale.

It wasn't until one afternoon, while perched on the toilet seat in the men's room at my job, I made the discovery that put things in a prospective order. Beside me in an unorganized array was junk mail, newsletters, job memos, discarded work orders, and trivial bullshit of every kind. Needless to say, the employees of the factory were not very selective with their reading materials. This was after all the decade leading to the great pulp and watershed of paper products that were said to be diminishing our rainforests and cluttering our street and sewers. Earth Day became a yearly observance that year, along with the concerned citizen's raid on city halls across the boroughs, ranting about noise pollution and crime. It was here on a tilted stack of Sears catalogs and work–boot ads that an old copy of Playboy magazine illuminated the debris. Despite being torn and ragged, a few months outdated and falling apart with the centerfold missing, it was still sturdy enough to leaf through for some editorial news of the day. It is amazing to look back on how we got our news and entertainment in those days—pre-computer, that is—from diners' club and sophisticated men-smoked pipes. Car ads, elaborate stereo systems, swanky men's shops built a legacy for a marketing genius that created an empire on bunny outfits and swimming pool parties.

There was an ad wedged between a Pan Am stewardess and an Italian bootmaker that caught my eye, nearly rocking me off my ceramic deficatorium.

It was a quarter-page clip of a man propped up on the floor stroking the carpet. He had a devilish look in his eye that was to imply he was not alone, luring the viewer to join him—obviously one of the chosen winners of his time: a ladies' man, cool breeze, a real finger-popping' daddy. The ad was in bold black-and-white romantic cursive lettering. It read, "The Swangarden Love Rug."

Only the best hotels supply it. Once you feel the sensuous delight of the furry "Love Rug," you will never go back to ordinary again. The incredible fibers will stroke your feet from heel to toe. The love rug is beautiful to look at. Only another animal of its stripe can tell it wasn't real. Specialty carpeting in minx, lynx, or jaguar.

"Swangarden Carpets: We Ain't Just Shag"

My jaw dropped. The man was famous. That ad must have cost him a pretty penny. I wondered if "Hef" himself had his carpeting all about the mansion: the Swangarden compound, the three coins in a fountain, the three little bears.

Lydia's stepmother Vivian, as mentioned, was a real piece of work; a snappy, foul-mouthed old school cookie. She smoked, played pool, and wore a girdle that outlined her generous curves. There were rumors that she drank like Ava Gardner. A real Sinatra style "broad" hot for those days. Greek, I believe. Her father owned a string of diners.

The new rich coming into my town; things were changing forever.

I suppose neighbors thought of me as a quiet young man—he goes to work every day, pays his taxes, listens to his father's music, and parts his hair on the side. Not many folks in my neighborhood knew I existed. Except for an occasional trot to the store, I mostly kept to myself.

One afternoon Lydia was carrying a tray of food from the old man's car to her yard. She pretended not to know me. The Swangardens were throwing a drunker-than-hell bacchanal in their yard, and Lydia was there with her boyfriend, Glen—a real knucklehead from the neighborhood. I suppose now in retrospect he was probably the flavor of the week. She was always with the coolest guy ever—by high school standards, the norm for the day—or at least I thought so. But then again, in retrospect, looking back over my four-decade-plus fantasy-fatigued memories, I recognize how old Lydia picked her boyfriends with the same critical criteria she used in selecting her underwear—going for style, popularity, and brand as opposed to quality, substance, and stain resistance.

Once again, fate intervening, a summer breeze blows a flower from her hair directly into my path; I ran over to pick it up and brought it to her. Her arms full of Corelle baking dishes plumping her breasts up accentuating her cleavage, I was unable to speak.

She crouched slightly forward and said, "Oh, thank you. Will you be a sweetheart and just stick that up here? I will straighten it out later."

She always had this false way of talking when she was around older men; a guttural flirty tone exaggerated like a film star or something, a natural gift for playing into the camera and men's eyes.

She probably thought I was a boy from the neighborhood because of my diminutive stature and youthful face. Even at twenty-seven, I was unable to grow a full beard.

Before me was a coif of scented hair made fragrant with floral shampoo, with two carnations affixed to it. I reached over, ever so delicately, almost in slow motion as I placed the flower back with the others.

"Thanks," she said and scudded away in quick little steps as to not drop her tray, her buttocks undulating beneath her dress like fleshy jellyfish swimming away.

Lydia! Oh, Lydia! Say, have you met Lydia?

Back in the days of my boring evenings, I studied journalism at night. I entertained a dream of breaking out of the nipple foundry forever and doing something cool and rewarding with my life… like Walter Cronkite or something. It was a good time in life when the classroom was full of impressionable and idealistic young journalists; letters were long as moon-eyed poets shed verse onto blank and ordinary pages that went on and on. In all honesty, I must confess, there has been nothing extraordinary in the circumstances under which I have come to know and be smitten by Lydia.

I will refrain from using the word love as well as the name Lydia because I have been devoid of both—the emotion (love) and Lydia (thy bitter name)—for some time now. So, in preserving my present stable health, I will refer to her only as L from here on in.

I can't recall with any great accuracy when my beloved L first possessed my reasoning, but I am aware of when we first became aware of our mutual feelings toward each other.

As the weeks rushed by, the months seemed to drag; L was learning to drive. As a gift, her father presented her with a late model Ford Mustang which was all the rage at the time. It would only make sense that I could help her with her driving lessons. She had a permit to drive, provided that she was accompanied by a licensed driver. I was Johnny on the spot.

It did not take long for me to realize that L already knew a thing or two about where to park. I have to admit I felt uncomfortable about making out in the car at the ripe old age of twenty-seven, about to turn twenty-eight. L, however, was extremely excited about it, always wanting to explore.

L began to hit the heights (literally and figuratively) of popularity with her friends and the type of exciting boys a Ford Mustang could attract. Most were local yokels that would pose no threat to our relationship, although I secretly hoped something would change.

I rushed the months to go quickly so L would turn eighteen, thereby reducing the stigma attached to our age difference and, thus, causing a decrease in surveillance from my inquiring neighbors. However, some things distracted me from my course of action.

In those next few weeks, I was becoming more comfortable with L as I learned more about her. Our time away from my hurried uncomfortable garage to solemn quiet moments at our make-out spot opened a new dimension of understanding to me. We had never gone to a motel; I could not make that leap; although L in her suggestive way hinted toward it.

I see now my denial—the cloudy illusion of my ego and sheer vanity, for lack of a better term—was enabling L to use me as a learning tool. I believe now that she needed to be savvy in other parts of her life for her plans; she needed coaching and didn't want to suffer the stigma of whoring with the local boys, a fast-track course she would not get at home or school. My honest temperament and discreet lifestyle were perfect for her to have her way with me; I never suspected I was being used because she never asked for anything... except for anatomy lessons.

Our conversations would veer off quickly. The most enduring part of our dialogue was about her future plans. She spoke of modeling at one point, and then of acting. Her father was dead against both because of the reputation it had; not to mention he was grooming her to step into the carpet business being she was his only heir. There were other options available to him; the options were taken off the table. For instance, L had two stepbrothers both from Vivian's former marriage. Both turned out to be wayward slackers. They lived with their father Vivian's former husband in California. They were not extended members of the Swangarden family because of an incident Involving L.... That is all I know of the matter and all I wanted to know. L at fourteen was five foot eight and developing rapidly; she showed me photos. This was at her home in California before they made the move East. She was stunning by the poolside.

There was a photographer friend of Herbert's that showed more than an interest in L, and possible career goals for the young princess. He had connections with a playboy mansion and knew people of influence ... There were rebellious arguments rumors of running away...The family left and moved east.

I was never jealous of any of L's male friends, I did feel a slight angst over a young man who was making the scene lately. A different type; longhair and shady, a stereotype of what was being deemed as the new romantic in those days. He was always hanging around in one way or another. He would never go by the house; father would never approve. So, they would meet at different points I know because I followed.

Getting back to this box on the table.

Curiously, this delivery came on the heels of her cremation. Fate seems to behave like that. I have a suspicion that someone or something is watching; an invisible third person, me, myself, and I (eye), as Lauren used to say. The mind's eye personified; the adult fixing thing in our heads—putting it all in order because we are sloppy children.

Here again, I begin to feel that peculiar notion as if someone is watching; not just a mild paranoia that sometimes occurs, but the distinct chill of something or someone familiar. It is difficult to explain; it is a kind of darkness associated with new beginnings. As though this thing (strange, I said a thing) is trying to enter from the outside of me. I feel I am giving birth to a new sensation. Almost orgasmic in its onset, it fills me with supernatural awareness I cannot describe; like being able to see beyond a dark road of opposites.

Lydia wrote me a note a long time ago. It frightened me to this day. I have thought about it in intervals over time. It was shortly after being pulled into her confidence that she began to share with me her ideas on death and the afterlife—and again of the presence of another; on that issue, however, she was reluctant to speak. Something held her back. A black discipline seemed to take hold of her. I felt it also. I feared for her this one particular episode, she would pass out from choking; her spasms were so intense as though something choked her from the inside, twisting her violently; her eyes were rolled back, exposing only the whites as if seized by convulsion; then it never happened that way again. It was that one and only time.

However, on the train, while en route to the crematorium, it came at me again in a bit of a different way; I had not had a clear thought in many months, but this I recall. It went something like this:

> There were two earthly phantoms pressed in the womb.
>
> Radiant with an inner light, they projected.
>
> In one, there was an earthly princess dressed in gauze cotton with a plaid shawl wrapped tightly around her shoulders.
>
> The other begot a gray ashen smock, along with an old death wrap tunic that swathed about her loins— bruised and shriveled.
>
> Her eyes were blue-black; the luster of coal. She is terrible to behold.
>
> She watches closely and mocks; "Sure of your body, I will be."

L told me that she never felt alone. She had no fear of death because death was with her, always watching.

I wrote it off and paid it no mind; it was typical of the death-wish messages that were prevalent in those days, brought on, most likely, by some rock lyric or a heavy metal band.

That ghastly day; how I found out about Lydia's passing—Beth, my dear old sister, of course; she found out about it. Her investigative little network of cronies from the old neighborhood who have been archiving neighborhood events, past and present, for thirty-odd years.

"Oh, Beth do you remember so-and-so…"

"They were just divorced from—"

"Yes, he is a big lawyer now…"

"That little store on the corner… yes…"

"Oh! Lydia… Lydia Swangarden. That tall girl. Monte's friend, wasn't it? She had that gland problem, grew to be almost seven feet tall. Moved away years ago, yep! Semi-pro wrestling… How a nice boy like Monte ever got involved with that wild woman…"

"Died, uh… Huh, poor thing. I heard from Pam that the medical report was that her heart could not support her size… The coffin was the size of a canoe."

There was a joke someone told me at Klosky's bar and grill once: big woman, little hole; a little woman is all hole. He was a veteran from the conflict in Korea. The women were slight in stature there.

What triggered his sense of humor was that Lydia came into Klosky's one evening to get a pack of cigarettes from the vending machine for her stepmother, who was rumored to be dying from emphysema. This was all well after we had broken up our secret romance and gone our separate ways. Lydia was about twenty-five at this time and well over the six-foot-seven mark. My sneering acquaintance leaned into me and whispered with distilled bar breath. "She dates old men. You know Sam Costello at the station? He goes with her. He has got to be over fifty."

I slinked back inwardly feeling a little embarrassed of my past escapade, wondering if he had known anything about us; if, maybe, he heard something on the street and was mocking me… maybe saw me around back in the day. That is how things work in the community. Old scouts like this guy never leave; they are a sentinel. I am sure I twitched, maybe even blinked once or twice nervously. However, looking over at him, I sensed no suspicion that he was malicious of me. His dull glazed eyes just stared straight ahead like Pavlov's dog, mechanically lifting his beer, sipping on cue whether he was thirsty or not. I soon let it go.

Come to think of it, the last time I saw ole lady Swangarden was a hot summer day; she was meandering around the patio. She was hooked up to an oxygen tank, the kind you could wheel around on some kind of hand jack. She was wearing a robe, emaciated as hell. The wind blew her robe open; her loose-fitting bloomers were hanging off her dehydrated torso. Her tits were yellow sacks of cornmeal. Herbert was gone, Lydia was gone, and I thought she was abandoned to suffer that tank by herself. Kind of cruel; I thought that no one gave a shit about her. Then someone came out of the house—a caretaker, I guess—scolding her and removing something from her stubborn hand, probably cigarettes. After some pushing and shoving, the caretaker escorted her back inside. I guess someone has to be around in case the old bag drops dead or blows up the oxygen tank with a lighted match. Trying to light up by an oxygen tank…

When I decided to go to the cremation service, I had just gotten off the phone with my sister Beth. She was in cahoots with her daisy chain of neighborhood scamps who gave her the scoop on everything over the last twenty-odd years. Of course, these were facts in bits and pieces taken from sources of second and thirdhand rumors.

Everyone who had ever lived in the neighborhood over the past four decades had some gossip to contribute concerning the Swangardens.

News about them was passed from generation to generation like they were celebrities. It was no surprise that Herbert Swangarden was a big fish in a small pond and he liked it that way. He could get things done more easily, shucking and jiving city officials which he did constantly (when he wasn't pushing his neighbors around).

Ole Vivian was popular with the charity fundraisers and the civic event crowd even though nobody wanted her around. Her chain-smoking brought with its fits of coughing and wheezing; combined with her foul language and devil-may-care attitude, she was quickly becoming an embarrassment to the local prim-and-proper auxiliary gals who found her to be cramping their style with her rude insouciance.

Not much was brought up about Lydia. It seems she just drifted into obscurity after her wrestling college days waned.

Having moved out of town and changed her name several times for professional reasons, no one really knew what to make of her, and she was soon forgotten. She never married; that much everyone could reasonably surmise. She did come to settle somewhere in Texas; that much was known.

Beth's friend, Sylvia, still worked at a postal station by the old city hall. There was a fuss being made over a large box that came in airfreight overnight and was to be delivered to the Rigby and Jeremiah Funeral Home. It was being shipped from a Texas central station to Newark, New Jersey, where it was going to be transferred by truck to Little Ferry, New Jersey, where Rigby and Jeremiah were going to pick up the delivery. The contents posted for delivery was Lydia Swangarden / proper remains. Signed, sealed, delivered.

It was one of those days; I stepped off the train into a miserable downpour that lasted the rest of my stay. I made it to Rigby and Jeremiah's funeral service center, repelling slants of rain that were hammering my hat and coat. Within an inch of drowning while standing up, I trotted into the lot and took a moment's refuge behind a barbican gate that was left partially opened; nestling beneath a brown cinder block enclosure with an overhanging roof, I rested momentarily to examine my surroundings. There was a simple wooden tower extending from the building with a small shutter window; affixed to the roof, a weather vane blew wildly against the wind. To my left was a dumpster painted industrial green.

There it was, the dilapidated cardboard box drenched and collapsing in the rain; letters running down the side in thick indelible ink. Human remains of Lydia Swangarden. Air freight stickers were stamped and about Paris, Texas. Handle with care. The carton, if not squelched by the rain, would have been the size of a refrigerator had the rain not collapsed it. Why was it there in plain sight? Why was it not disposed of properly so visitors to the funeral service would not see it? It was empty; just packing remains thrown inside, packets of what might have been ice or something jumbled in plastic. The Undertaker might have momentarily abandoned it because of the sudden rain. My eyes kept falling back to that label.

Paris, Texas—a horror shot through me. L used to constantly clamor on about going to Paris (France) to be a star in foreign films. As always, she pursued this dream passionately. After some costly acting lessons and a brief stint at a swanky academy abroad, a disillusioned and lonely puppy returned home with some tattered luggage and her tail between her legs. When she began growing almost a yard taller than the average French actor, she let it go saying, "Maybe I will go to Paris, Texas; I hear everything in Texas is big… like me. Maybe I am just misplaced."

Lydia, oh, Lydia.

I looked up at the tower, then across the yard to the main building of the cremation facility; a much larger matching tower loomed in the foggy distance. Some smoke was making its way through the flute. What the hell; I may as well watch it from here rather than make a spectacle of myself by showing up late and soaking wet.

The chances of me knowing anyone inside are slim to zilch. I cannot think of who would have attended. Besides, I feel a sense of closeness next to this packing crate; the holy sarcophagus that ushered that once magnificent friend—yes, this is palpably more comforting to be here in the rain alone with this talisman and memory than to watch a phony coffin go up in smoke.

I can distinguish the single stream of tear on my cheek warmer even than the rain that covered my face because my tear is salty over my lip; how magical I found her final resting place in the rain, over two hundred miles of traveling on buses and trains to get here. Not to mention the waiting.

Let me be clear about waiting. I have always been an impatient man. I suppose it is part of my neurosis. No one likes to think of a behavioral quirk common to many as a neurotic symptom. Dr. Vlad—Father Vladimir, I should say, my priest/therapist)—said that I think too much; I should slow down the mental pictures in my brain. Maybe try meditation or prayer. As a result, all I have managed to do was procrastinate better. I have waited for the good, and I have waited in vain, but always I have waited in hope.

Father Vlad is a good man; he talks to me pro bono because I am too broke to afford a real shrink. However, I believe he gets it; we talk mostly about sex although he has never banged a woman in his life…

As I already mentioned, the art of waiting was confusing to me. Why would God not just give you what you are destined to have? With so many variables life has to offer, we must wait for the sand to settle naturally before a simple pool of water on the beach becomes clear again. Thank you, Lauren.

More than that, it is probably a test of free will. God, it seems, is big on this free will thing. We are only allotted a little portion of time out of all eternity while every silly, useless thing chips away at it little by little and accomplishes nothing.

I am forever waiting in line at the supermarket. Bus lines, airports, and phone calls—these are designated to measure virtue; if you fail at one of these, you will never wait long enough for your ship to come in. Ha! The only sure wait is the one for Godot, who eventually always shows up.

Lydia.

Having decided to wait it out I watched the visitors leave one by one—not many as I had thought. There was an odd man who stood out; off to the side and alone. I thought, at first, he was a driver or undertaker of some sort, but no. He was tall and svelte in appearance and bore a resemblance to Vincent Price with his noir umbrella and silver hair and mustache. I can't help thinking I have seen him before, maybe in a movie or a train terminal. He looked the type to be the guy you would see sitting on a bench at the bus depot getting a two-bit shoe shine. Something about him was familiar, although I am sure we have never met. I have seen that face before. That being said, a curious couple that was the last to exit distracted my attention. A man being wheeled out with what looked like an intravenous apparatus rolling along next to him was being carefully loaded into a van by a young woman dressed in black with a mourner's veil, along with another person that could have been an orderly or nurse.

Is that the old man? Who is the babe in black?

Her father, Herbert Swangarden, is still alive. The carpet magnate, the one with all the dough ray, me, escarole, cheddar? Christ, he must be ancient. I remember how he threatened me to stay away from Lydia; accused me of provoking her. Me! Now that I think back, I should have had better constraint, but Lydia was no child at seventeen—far from it. If he only knew how she threw herself around at older men! If I had only known at the time; imagining I was special. What a fool I was. Swangarden Carpets: "We Ain't Just Shag"—indeed.

There was at least one eye witness to the fact that on more than one occasion Lydia prompted the groundskeeper, an ancient and balding drunk, to "tickle her provocatively," - according to Mrs. Hennesy, who caught them flirting while spying out her window—with a pair of binoculars, I might add; she, in turn, passed the gossip on to the spinster kemp woman where it trickled down that venomous path, snowballing until it eventually led to sister Beth who dropped it on me.

Mrs. Hennesey was kept indoors due to a huge growth on the side of her neck. It was of the sort that stretched the skin across its surface, drawing attention to a network of veins and capillaries that radiated from underneath. Due to the pressure, it grew into a bulbous deformity that sprang from her thyroid; a glandular disorder causing her eyes to bulge from their sockets—a condition that left her self-conscious about her appearance. All of this was accentuated by a pair of large framed bifocals that caused her eyes to appear even more grotesque than they already were; watery pale blue and bloodshot.

Despite her maladies, her eyesight remained intact—at least well enough to keep up with her duties as a self-appointed neighborhood watch. The Hennesy's attic window faces the tail end of the Swangardens sprawling yard, a gazebo, and flower shed was where the episodes of Lydia being felt up by the old gardener took place.

You see, if you live somewhere long enough, you become part of the mosaic composition; through osmosis, you become like the cars and tenement stairwells. The smell of the cooked meals and the whispering behind closed doors; the girl upstairs prepping for a date and the junkie in the basement. By day, you absorb the toxins around you; by night, you expel poisons in the form of fresh and innocent dreams. Fairies whitewash your fences. No one interferes with the scenery. The quiet loathsome activity of eavesdropping and coveting is sweeter than that the chirping of the birds.

Fences make good neighbors.

Lydia, oh, Lydia.

It wasn't until years later when I ran into Mr. Swangarden at a local store; all was forgotten by then, and in fact, he had difficulty remembering me. Lydia was quite grown and moved on with her career. She was in the car—backseat driver's side; she slid out on to curbside, almost banging her head.

She had the girlish innocent face of an angel with the body of a runway model on steroids. She stayed slightly crouched to bring our heights into a more reasonable perspective. I had not seen her for many years. I was older and slightly balder. Standing as straight as I could, trying to project as much height as humanly possible; the best I could do was come up to just below breast level. She was looming magnificently like a Las Vegas billboard.

We spoke by the car for a while as she told me how she was embraced by the wrestling industry as a top contender for the champion of the American Women's Wrestling Association (AWWA). She was the youngest ever to be considered for title bout—a notable swift accomplishment—after just recently coming out of wrestling college. If she defeats Baby Girl Thelma from Utah, she will clinch the title. She showed me a picture from a recent tabloid.

I could not believe my eyes. Was this my L? The photo showed a laminated tabloid photo of L. She was wearing tight-fitting leather pants. With a tacky lame gold jacket and high-heeled sneakers; her face was twisted in bizarre contortion as she appeared to be shouting down Baby Girl Thelma from across the ring. It was then that I first found out about the wrestling career. I had no idea Lydia Swangarden had carved fame and notoriety for herself as "Atlantis Obscura," the gorgeous amazon woman from New Jersey.

What was it with this place where so many suffered from bizarre glandular problems?

The electrical overhead grids that crisscrossed the sky that kept the clouds out?

The tank farms that stored chemical products?

And now Lydia was a curiosity to be reckoned with too.

I must make her into something so I can cope. Something I can slow down.

I have had it. She was a pendulum, a great clock that just pushed forward with fads and perspectives. "Today, wrestling; tomorrow, the world."

I remember feeling small now, emotionally crippled. Not so much that I had envy for L. I had none. It was for my shortcomings and lack of courage to face the world that I had an issue with; not having anything to say for myself in the afterglow of everyone else's success around me that made me self-conscious.

To hear she had successfully moved on—be it only a cheesy vain venue; a glamour stunt—it was a move in a direction; it was my nightmare to have her go forward.

My relationship with L was a stepping stone in her life. I had not progressed at all.

I began dating Lauren soon after we fell out—and wishy-washy about it, I might add. I had not even thought of bringing my relationship with Lauren up to L. Shouldn't that have been a red flag? That I was not proud enough of my relationship with Lauren to mention it to L as a conversation piece? Here I am stunted, still at the foundry, pounding away at the brass nipples.

Did I not know that my relationship with Lauren was a farce, a phony fraud? Did I marry Lauren to have something to talk to Lydia about if we should ever meet again?

Not too much to say.

I said that if I could, I would make Lydia into a grand old clock; therein might be the answer.

I believe that by watching Lydia expel her youth before me, I might live through her; she, as always, was the big hand on a tower clock quickly spending the unnoticed minutes. I, as the little hand, was drudgingly recording the hours.

It was not without some envy that I could admire the way she took chances because, after all, time and resources were all on her side.

I play it safe. I let time gently change the tides for me, bringing me safely and predictably back home. But for Lydia, oh, Lydia—the clock forges only forward. If the only regret was a clock to be turned off and on; backward and forward. Regrets and time would still pass, but not record.

> Clocks that tick, chime, and ring;
> Clocks that echo bellow and sing;
> Clocks with patience and pendulums swing road-
> faced and numbered with old dusty springs.

Clocks in the corners of clandestine halls;
Clocks hang like sentinel paintings on walls.
In dusty vapidity of tapestry halls,
The clangor of clocks as the new hour falls.
Clicking so slightly ever so lightly;
Clocks in the chambers; hidden by doors.
In cathedrals and towers on prominent squares...
Old Byzantine mortar embedded in shale.
Clocks old and broken in attics and rooms
Dull sinister casements in vacated tombs
With bulbous glass portals grotesque and unriveting;
while the hands of the clocks just keep pivoting and pivoting.
Turning and turning grossly unnerving... sand pebbles falling with each spin of the hand.
Clicking and cricketing, redundantly digiting...
I have turned Lydia into a clock. Big Banshee; she was emboldened by time.

If I could make such a personification that Lydia was a measurement device, a timepiece of culture, I would make her a towering clock; she was big like America—a zeitgeist. She would always fit in, find a niche; the eternal girl out of place. She could roll over you and change your lifestyle. She could bring you into focus or distort you completely. I cannot see her as a woman ever, despite her size and age lines forming around her eyes and a slight chicken neck developing around her throat.

It was during her wrestling career that she became fascinated with playing the drums. She had met a Japanese martial arts wrestler named Nanon Moon who fronted a female rock band called the Moon Geishas. Lydia changed her name again to Zildgen Cross. The band consisted of Nanon Moon, singer; Zoey, the astrological zodiac girl on guitar and keyboards; and Roxanne, Bonfire on Bass; along with Lydia—"Zildgen Cross"—the drummer. Three members were Japanese of normal height, except for Lydia. Their music menu consisted of songs written by bandleader Nanon Moon, which was mostly primal screaming and obscure dreamy lyrics. Nanon herself was an infamous lesbian in the club circuit. The band became popular at a seedy little showcase called the Ginger Lounge.

Everything was fine for those days; all the pieces right where they should be.

A little bit about the Ginger Lounge.

In the early days of burlesque decades before, it was a popular nightclub that featured only redhead singers and dancers. As the neighborhood declined, the swank hotels and restaurants turned into flophouses and liquor stores. As further decay set in, the low rents brought all kinds of slum lord activity such as drug dens and homeless hotels. The custodian at the Ginger Lounge's main job was to keep the street and the bathrooms clean. Outside, the blood and urine ran like a stream from an alley that separated the Ginger Lounge from the Royalty Hotel—a men's homeless shelter.

The proprietor of the Ginger Lounge was Carlyle Hildebrandt, the youngest of the Hildebrandt boys, whose family owned a string of apartment buildings on the lower east side.

As the properties slowly got liquidated and sold off, Carl held on to an old storefront property and turned it into a bar nightclub, featuring local entertainment and cheap booze. The low rent and seediness attracted a new style element of the street performer—the folk singer. The political scene was ripe for anarchy and all kinds of expatriates, and weekend revolutionaries piled in from the suburbs from all across the fruited plain. Every Tuesday and Friday night, the fabulous Moon Geishas hauled their equipment over and performed. All went well, until once upon a promise, Carlyle on a whim with Nanon told her he would manage their band and bring in some record people in hopes of getting them signed to a record deal. Zoey the astrological Zodiac girl protested, insisting that with mercury in retrograde, something sinister was about to develop and they should not do it. She was partly right.

Carlyle had agents from Dish Records coming in, that was true. But it was to see another band that was featured on the card that night Carlyle had an interest in—not the Moon Geishas. He was using the Moon Geishas in name only because of their strength in drawing the better audience. When they found out there was a real shit show, Lydia kicked Carlyle Hildebrandt in the face with a sweeping roundhouse fracturing his left eyebrow. She was wearing a man's size eleven and a half steel-tipped jackboots.

This pretty much put the kibosh on Lydia's drumming career.

It is two o'clock in the afternoon, and I am breaking up my weekly chat with Father Vlad.

"Those were the days. Father, if I dare say, if you had known Lydia as I knew Lydia, you might not be wearing that collar today."

A gentle laugh. "Monte, thank you for speaking with me today; I think a little spiritual encouragement might do you good."

"That, and maybe bourbon or two. Let me ask you something, Brother. Why was it that Christ turned water into wine and then stopped? I mean he could have a produced a kick-ass bourbon if he wanted to."

Brother Vlad smiled and scratched his chin, blue eyes twinkling behind a rubicund jowl.

"That I would have to think about; however, the Chinese have a saying: 'A man becomes the room he is in.' I would have to say—being a Jesuit immersed in many philosophies, it is my humble opinion—I would have to conclude there were probably no Irish men in the Middle East at that time. Also, stay away from that bourbon, my boy; alcohol is a depressant, and we are trying to lift your spirits internally, not dull them."

Monte cast an eye over Dr. Vlad (Brother Vlad) for the first time with an air of comely gratitude and respect. With a sincere curiosity that was somewhat alien to Monte (who for the most part was always teetering on defensive, rude, and miserable), he asked a straight-out question.

"I am curious about people like you, Brother. You left a country that was war-torn and starving; learned several languages, you moved around the world and settled here in the refurbished basement of an old church on its last legs, opting for a life of devoted poverty in a country that could offer you a fortune with your brains and gift for learning. What gives? With a little anger and some grit, a guy like you could climb pretty swiftly. I have been working with the same brass nipple company my whole life and am ignorant as to just how one goes about traveling. I can't even leave my crummy apartment for a decent vacation. I would like to pick your brain, Brother; what makes a guy like you tick?"

The silence that ensued was thick like a Belgian fog. Vlad sat back and clasped his fingers. His slack jaw hung as a slight quiver along his jowls caused a pocket of loose flesh to tremor just under his chin.

He stared just past Monte into a reverent space. He did not nictitate; exhaling with a sigh that was neither despondent nor remorseful. He spoke the following.

"I came from a small village; I don't recall the name of it. I was very young at the time, and such things did not matter. The people of the village were beyond wretched. It was cold; I remember being ill with fever—somewhat hallucinogenic, I believe. My family did a little better than most; we had firewood and some tools. Food was a miracle every day.

My father raised some small animals and was clever enough to breed them instead of selling them. I think I might have had siblings; there was a girl and a little boy older than me. No matter how hard I try I cannot remember them. Only that they were slim, nightmarish apparitions of bone and cloth.

Something happened, something terrible. Everyone was killed. Kidnapping the village young for their meat was practiced openly by some barbaric hordes that lived further up in the mountain regions where food was nonexistent. The younger siblings might have been boiled for their flesh. I was left to die because of the fever; I was tainted. The illness saved my life.

Some Jesuits that raised me later rescued me. I do not know any other life. This is my earliest and only childhood memory. Nevertheless, from what I have witnessed from other villages, I had to do service—I realize I was not any different from many of these unfortunate rustics. The only thing that separated us was luck... or some say the divine. I like to believe in miracles. I am in the industry."

He smiled and let go of a laugh, whether forced or genuine; it tightened the loose skin around his face making him appear somewhat jocular, like a Franz Hals painting. "I think I will have a taste of that bourbon now, if the offer still stands."

I poured a generous serving into a plastic cup, and we talked for a little while longer. When I left for my bus, I felt drained somewhat, as if a superior had humbled me. I could not place the emotion. I only knew that, at that moment, I respected Vlad more than I had respected anyone ever in my life.

Back at the bus depot, the warm bourbon is relaxing for me. My mood was shifting. I could not think of how these sessions with Vlad were helping—sure I feel good for a little while, but again the loneliness sets in.

Now it is the ants.

Waiting again, nothing left to do but relax my mind; sitting on an old concrete bench, feeling my ass adapt to the cold. Thinking of that story by Brother Vlad and not quite feeling the cold that much anymore.

The old wives' tale comes to mind: "Don't sit on the cold concrete you will get hemorrhoids. Piles, as they say, another extinct and forgotten colloquialism for the antediluvian dung heap."

Where did I hear that? Was it Mom, after all? The same wise woman who told my sister, "If you want to move quickly, take my advice—pull down your bloomers and slide on the ice." The poetry— now I know where I get it from.

I could not help thinking if Vlad's mother would have told him anything like that—if there had been more time; if things were different.

There was no one around the depot. I am wondering how the ants know when to come out. I am not sure if I am daydreaming or not.

I looked down and noticed a team of ants pulling larvae along a crack in the pavement squares. They were a tiny medieval procession of peasants dragging a boar back to the village. The larva was alive and fighting to resist.

I am looking closer now, and on further inspection, the larvae turned out to be a common maggot.

I watched on and despite the twisting and turning and furious effort to escape by the maggot, it was futile. That healthy plump maggot about to give birth to a fly was easily twice the size of one ant.

It was overpowered and outnumbered. Not unlike Roman soldiers prodding Christ through Calvary to the hill of skulls. The ants managed to tire out the creature at least four times.

This brought to mind a wonderment I experienced as a child as to why Christ could not smite the Roman soldiers with his supernatural powers. Could he not get angry like the Hulk? Or use some kind of ray-like the Green Lantern? Brother Vlad reminds me, be mindful that the history was written by Apostles and not a genius comic book writer. Besides if Christ was to unleash supernatural power and the good guys win… we would not have faith, would we?"

Have? Or *need*, I wonder?

Anyway, getting back to Lilliputian ants and their Gulliver, the ants somehow hoisted the larvae over lower ants positioned beneath it, managed to elongate the larvae and secure it; and then managed to carry it along to their lair.

The battle for life by the larvae was horrifying, increased with the intensity brought on in dreams. But I am wide awake. It was clear the ants had the advantage of utilizing speed, number, and superior strength… and a well-rehearsed plan. The larva, although wiry with twisting agility, had no arms and was blind. It was defeated by sheer force and number; not to mention the ant's unrelenting collective will to conquer its prey.

I can't bear them. They are killing me. All this exposure is killing me. She is killing me. What does she want—what?

Does she want me to celebrate life? She is too foreign, untranslatable—I have to get out of here.

I get to my door I can barely open it. The key fell twice. Everything is the same. That hideous box is still on the table. Open it; go ahead. What are you going to find? She is dead and with her died all the secrets.

I can't right now, I must lay down. This whole day has been a weight so far. I should have went to work—the pounding of those machines.

Everyone moves around. I have been pumping out brass nipples for years—heavy crates, forklifts. Two weeks' vacation; for what? This bed is like a crucible.

Okay, let's clear my head; calm, breath.

Bless me, father, for I have sinned.

I stole a banana and ate the skins.

Is it unholy to summon the dead?

What would I say if I was interviewing with her before the golden gate tribunal?

Suppose I was interviewing her for the hereafter. Just before death. The last few minutes before the brain synapses burn out. Lydia laid out comatose unable to control anything and *wham*! I pop into her head like a cartoon character; Lichtenstein yellow exploding in primary colors, moving within the tiny black dots.

Me: "So let's get to know Lydia. Why are you not wrestling so much these days? Or better yet—why are you not playing in a band? I thought the artistic solace would be good for you at this stage of your life."

L: "I was finding it more and more difficult to express myself through wrestling. And then there is the age issue; I cannot do this forever. I am sorry to sound so cliché, but it is true. My audience has outgrown the need for my particular brand of symbolism. The onslaught of social and digital media has rendered all I have to express visually useless. Very few people care about the symbols. Female wrestling is all about images and symbols. Imagination is tainted—sometimes fantastic—and a tremendous liar. I don't think it is malicious; just childlike in its wants and needs.

Sometimes, in the ring, I am a superhero; I cannot project myself as a regular person. A simple piece of candy can satisfy a rambunctious child, and sometimes the thought of how Monte would fondle me through my panties on an elevator could be enough to seduce my insecurities with our relationship."

Me: "Really? Who is Monte—your lover?"

L: "Lover is such a trite expression. In my world, there are only muses. I suppose you could say he is a muse of the highest order. Let's just say, before Monte, it did not seem possible for me to envision a man and a woman loving each other deeply."

Me: "You sound not only angry, but something more. You look uninterested. You sound and look like you are enraged."

L: "I am; I would like to kill him."

Me: "Do you feel impotent—about taking action I mean? You seem to feel impotent."

L: "I am."

Me: "Impotence usually accompanies rage. What are you impotent about?"

L: "I can't get him to acknowledge me."

Me: "And you don't accept that."

L: "No."

Me: "And there is the intensity to your rage that seems to be greater than the situation calls for."

She pauses.

Me: "What are you experiencing?"

L: "A lot of men in my life who have been like that."

Me "Like your father?"

L: "You mean my real father, —the one who was married to my real mother. A pity she died so young—a fatal car crash. She was enraged that night after learning of father's affair with Vivian. She was on route to confront them; wasn't thinking, I guess. *Bang*! End of story. Francis Baker. Never got to know her."

Me: "A car crash? I see here in your bio something about her giving birth to twins—twin girls… There were two of you; you are aware of that, I am sure."

L: "No! No! We must stop this now! I know Mom blamed me for her death. Why should I have lived? I have always thought she is with me still, growing inside me; hoisting up above my shoulders. Maybe that is why I keep growing; her stillborn spirit is stretching us both upward to heaven… My invisible twin. My dark sister."

This isn't a shot in the dark. The work proceeds into experiencing the narcissistic injury from her father, who was never responsive to her.

She told me on several occasions that there was a stillborn death—a twin. L had never wanted to be the survivor; the selfish anger it caused her father towards her for killing her mother... his wife.

The tape in my recorder clicks then continues in silence. Seconds later, Lydia speaks.

"Why do I wrestle? Haha! Clouds are all about rain even when it is not raining. God is about competing even while he is quietly observing. A criminal is guilty even when he poses as a saint. Also, I am an athlete; I am competing even when...

I am down."

Why did I do it?

Lydia Swangarden.

A cool breeze is blowing in from the window. It must have been raining while I dozed off; I can feel cool sprinkles shaking on my skin.

My Faberge egg never to be held to be delicately handled—never to be tasted. Nothing human I can press to my cheek; no scent to permeate my senses. Persistence of memory only Dali might imagine.

Not even a perfumed letter or a signature in your
script.
Your corpse burning to ashes, return to the sun
Ceramic petals tempered by heat—untouchable—
only that true porcelain shell you exist behind.
I look on till my eyes melt.
The pixels that form your image excite me;
You are the opposite of transcendental perfection
The Buddha's flame that burns to dispense no heat;
in you burns all the thermal energy of the universe.
You are my Lydia, my Brenda, my anis, my muse.
In a flash, I was sober; don't know how long I have
been out. I don't remember drinking but I must have
been. I am half in the sunlight half in the rain. My glass
is half empty, half filled with champagne.

L had a strange quirk that would sometimes annoy me. She would pronounce words according to their phonetic sounds. Knife, for example, would be "ka-nife"; expressing the silent letter with exaggerated force. Phone would become "pa-hone," lasagna would be "la-zag-nee," and so forth and so on. I know it was cute a comic element of her youth; I, however, had no sense of humor. Ultra conservative, the "man," the frustrated failed journalist who saw no humor in any of it. When I would confront her with my adult righteousness, she would retort with quick answers like, "who is happier—me or you? Why should I read books that make me think too much? Why is it so important to be right all the time?" or, "The problem with you, Monte, is that you have only one dick." She would then part her legs exposing her garden of earthly delight and proclaim. "With this, I can get as many of those as I want."

I would laugh, of course; that was when I did feel the sword of castration hanging over me. She could make me laugh as long as I kept my emotions at bay. We would joke and laugh throughout the evening until a tide of reality came rushing forth reminding me that it was a school night and she had to get home; at which point my terrible thoughts of aging would descend with blades sharp as shark's teeth.

There it is—that clock again. Our moments being measured by the different places we were on time. Could I have loved her? I married my adult counterpart, Lauren. All the right ingredients—we were equal in every way. Correct anatomically and intellectually— incurably neurotic, the both of us. The popular song on the radio at that time was Macarthur Park.

> Someone left the cake out in the rain.
> I don't know if I can take it, because it took so long
> to make it,
> And I'll never have the recipe again.

I don't know if even Jimmy Webb fully understands those lyrics as I do—to watch something you have labored over dissolve right before your eyes. I mean, a love relationship is like a recipe, is it not? You have to measure the correct ingredients, set certain temperatures, add layers of things like frosting or whatever… so much care is in baking. Then, someone carelessly leaves the cake behind in the rain; not grasping how much time, love, and understanding the baker put into it. At some point, the sugary frosting begins to melt. All the soft spongy layers emulsify, dripping and collapsing under its weight. The delicate lettering on top is now blurred and awash, dripping into puddles flooding the pavement with food color—candy apple greens and reds.

Not so unlike love. Your ingredients are understanding and patience; love has a temperature also in a corresponding way. Your temperance in situations—how you master the psychology of another person's wants and needs while changing your faults and adjusting to discoveries about one's self. Psychologists and researchers have proposed several different theories of love to explain how love forms and endures. Love is a basic human emotion, but understanding how and why it happens is not necessarily easy—not unlike baking.

Romantic love generally involves a mix of emotional and sexual desire There is often, initially, more emphasis on the emotions than on physical pleasure. The ingredients should be remembered so as not to ruin the layers and frosting between and on top. The frosting must be smeared with acceptance—praise the good, accept the flaws, and provide the inspiration to change. Love is neither a moment nor a feeling; it is a multi-layered cake; it is the existence of togetherness. When cutting a cake, all your cuts will be diameters, which means all the cuts will be straight lines that pass through the center of the cake; however, abandoning it is a heartbreaking thing. It was left to decay by someone who cared; someone who wanted to bring something nice and special to the party. But instead, the party wasn't interested—and the cake was left out in the rain.

The toil, the precision, the measuring… all for naught.

Lauren Lucretia Smith.

Joylandia is the fictional name I have given the place Lauren and I once resided in. It wasn't a town, and it wasn't any tangible residence that one can easily identify. Joylandia was more of a place in the heart—an imaginary garden that greater and more creative minds than mine invent in stories and fairytales. I suppose Tristan and Iseult envisioned it with the delusion and contradiction of romantic love, a sustainable faith that arises from the Psyche with the power of religion to heal and inform.

Joylandia at its best offers you truth and realism in a very physical world while simultaneously presenting a mirrored false truth and surrealism in a phony illusionary world—at least in my dim-witted account of things. All good children want to grow up and live in Joylandia. It is a suburb of contradictions. It is the greenery on the other side of the fence.

Joylandia, on the other hand—the unhealthy version—destroys its natives by trapping them with a false sense of security. Not any different from any other form of convention—than any other American city, I suppose. Having not traveled much and had only worked at the brass nipple foundry my whole life, I am not one to judge honestly. The few places I have been outside my humble existence, however, all seem pretty much the same to me. I will refer to the city that I live in as Joylandia; I also refer to that neurotic place in my heart as Joylandia. Not its real name, of course, but the anonymity of a false name gives me courage.

Remember: I am a coward, never quite could move on. I remained a social dwarf my whole life. Joylandia eats people like me for lunch.

Lauren, however, has traveled quite extensively; her father was a military man, so the family was on the move from one military installation base to another. She had a fine education and was reared properly in every way. So it made no sense to Lieutenant Smith when she brought me to the family dinner announcing we had plans to be married. Lieutenant Smith wasted no time in taking me into his study after dinner for a friendly chat over bourbon and cigars.

"So, Monte, Lauren mentioned you are a journalist, a newsman—articles, media, and such?"

"No, sir, I am sort of in the middle of putting things together with that part of my career."

"Oh, still employed with the brass foundry? Brass nipples are disappearing, you know; alloys and metals are on the wane. PCP pipe is the future for most industrial plumbing nowadays—heavy plastics. Have you researched anything about plastic compounds in college?"

"No, sir, I just basically stuck with journalism…"

He cut to the quick while I was still in mid-sentence.

"Is there anything I should know, Monte?"

"Know, sir, such as… future plans, you mean?"

"Well, that would be a good start, but I was talking about maybe a travesty of misconduct of any sort; no pregnancy of any sort that we are beating around the bush about, is there?"

It was then that I knew what he had on his mind.

"Oh no, no, sir—nothing like that. We are just kind of in love."

He looked at me and shifted his eyes to the floor; looking up again, he rose and walked over to the window. I was hoping he would jump out; no such luck.

"Welcome to the family." He walked toward me and extended his hand. I didn't get the feeling he entirely believed it himself. Standing over me, he somewhat crowded me into my seat.

Still holding my hand in his, he looked down on to me. I felt I was looking into the eyes of Lyndon Banes Johnson; they sort of looked alike.

Do you know anything about the military, Monte?'

"No, sir, I can't say I do."

Of course. Well, before I was a lieutenant, I was a drill sergeant in the Marines. Do you know what that is, Monte?"

"No, sir, I can't really say for sure…"

Still holding my hand, I could feel his grip tightening. His face was a switchboard of quizzical smiles. I sensed a real frightening menace behind his glare.

"Of course, you don't. Well, we took young men like you—younger than you; boys, that's what they were—and turned them into men. One can change a boy into a man with tough love and excellent guidance; however, once the die is cast into a man's life, the option for change becomes narrow. Stubbornness takes root on sandy soil. You feel my hand on yours—I could crush your hand; that is from years of building strength. It is not easy for a man to relinquish that strength over a lifetime of having it serve him, and he submits to it accordingly. Are you following me, son? Families are like that also; it is not easy to give things up, like a daughter, for instance. You say you are in love. Love is a transient word. I believe you work hard; I believe you are a good man; my daughter would not have it otherwise. Am I clear on this?"

"I believe so… sir".

"You believe so."

"If, at some point, she chooses to terminate this engagement, I will side with her. She is my daughter, and I put my family before all conventional foolishness. Am I clear?"

At that point, the door swung open, and Mrs. Smith entered inviting us into the dining room for coffee and desserts. From the perspective of the entrance doorway to anyone looking in, it would appear that we were engaging in oral sex the way officer Smith swarmed over me still squeezing my hand. It was clear he intended to prove dominance, and my role was to submit or get the fuck out and do not come back. I do not believe that I was what he had in mind for his daughter. And history has proved him correct.

I had made up my mind that night that I probably would not marry Lauren.

However, over the days to come—as fate would have it—before I could find a way to get out of our engagement, Lieutenant Smith was smitten by a massive heart attack that threw him into the jaws of demise. He never fully recuperated and died.

With that fatal event, my plans with Lauren were pretty much sealed. I was going to be the new man in her life. And naturally, I—Monte, with the humble shoe size of eight-and-one-half inches C width; somewhat flat-footed by military standard—was called upon to service the Smiths and marry their only daughter Lauren Elisa Smith, thus, stepping into the Buick size shoebox of lieutenant Gerard Smith's size 12 double E military issue Oxford to serve God and country, but most of all, to love, honor, and serve with the power invested in pastor, chaplain John L. Ricard, United States Armed Forces; forevermore. Amen.

Things moved forward; the days turned into weeks. Date night in Joylandia with Lauren was a cultivating experience. Usual courting procedures, neurotic date nights, and college nostalgia were how we spent our time. Heavy petting and half a blow job were enough to keep a young man coming back with great expectations of the honeymoon.

In relationships of hypergamy where it is usually expected for the woman to marry up into a higher social class, I could not fully relate…backward, I could not relate; being the man in this case—climbing the ladder of Rapunzel's hair to breach her tower—I was the one to do all the social climbing.

Joylandia is also an amusement park of happy horse shit.

All the notions that made a catchy pop song were hatched in Joylandia. For instance, there is a town of Scarborough about an hour's drive west, and they have a Scarborough fair, and the Autumn nights are lightly scented with parsley, sage, rosemary, and Lauren who chose to wear a citrus and herb perfume that day; she was as tempting as a turkey dinner—I wanted to gobble her up.

We did travel a long and winding road that led us to a simple plank board house with two cats in the yard. We did experience the smoke from a fireplace pumping billows of countryside domestic bliss. Fodder for the emotions with fantasies of a good clean life thrown in for the fuck of it; Joylandia was a giant rolling billboard demonstrating the humble rewards of work and sacrifice.

Now, in retrospect, however, I can only feel a frustrating memory as I stand in the rain watching my Lydia go up in smoke.

As I get older—and I am tipping the chart; well into the latter half of my middle years (some might say, already on the downward slope of the proverbial hill)—I find Joylandia more isolated than ever. It has become easier to identify and navigate through with fewer embarrassments, guilt, and regret; and mental fatigue usually accompanies.

As I look back at the films, music, and fashion that shaped my time in Joylandia, I realize what cultural vampires Lauren and I had become. That whole interstice was more playing for the camera and pretending than true quest individuality and/or togetherness. The more our lush and adolescent culture nurtured us, the more we were absorbed by it. The diamond ring advertisement on the back of a magazine became the diamond ring; bad poetry about love became love; a sentimental love song became the way and means to the inevitable broken heart.

Let me explain to you Joylandia the best way I can. It is ideal; one of the many phony delusions that crowd and occupy the vacancies of a person's emotional landscape over the years.

I have named it Joylandia; after all, it is a place that you travel and explore. A modern sequel to the Odyssey. It is not permanent if you do not want it to be, and it is permanent if you allow it to be. You can go home, providing someone is at the shore waiting for you to return. Or you can die on the journey if the gods tire of you.

I have spent most of my social time isolated in this mindful community long enough to now look back on it with tenderness—separate and illustrated like an old travel map or atlas with bloodshot lines and highlights: tourists traps, hotels, and entertainment.

For example, as a young boy, I would daydream of fishing off a breezy shore. A palm tree with twisting branches near off would sway—there is always a sense of someone watching; who was it? Of course, it was I; always from a remote place and different time, perhaps the person I am now was watching then, older and wiser like a godhead—the father of myself. I felt hopeful and patient; there was no tomorrow or yesterday but only that clear moment, a harbinger of the present offering.

There was also another destination stop on that imaginary tourist map as well. It was me again; this time a swarthy man, palpably older than the boy in the first daydream, standing in the fore room of a simple cabin. My hair was slicked back tightly to my skull; the facial shadow was thickening around my chin as the trace of a mustache followed along my upper lip (I was never able to grow a full beard in real life). I was always dressed the same—wore a thick plaid shirt cuffs rolled up just so. I should mention the long wood table with some scattered bowls. I was not alone in this daydream—physically, I mean. There was always a woman—the same woman, always—for these continuing sequences began during and after Lydia and carried on well into my relationship with Lauren Smith.

What is odd is that my point of view in this daydream is once again that of a remote observer. That observer, who again is me and I am him (and we are all together), has never seen the face of this woman; her back always turned to him (my observer). Rolling waves of chestnut hair cascading along her back exemplified this succubus; a simple blouse—she is almost a replica of Lydia from the back, except for the hair color. Lydia's was somewhat lighter in tint, the natural bleaching effect brought on by ritual sun worshiping. This woman, however, might never have seen the sun; her skin was pale, like that of one who has never basked in earthly sunlight. But I, again, as the person in burly shirt, am experiencing this dual comparison; pondering the coincidence of how two women both created separately—one by nature and one a complete invention of my mind—could pull me in tow with a supernatural gravity that renders me defenseless.

I can recall only that she was a picture of loveliness... I choose my words carefully here for I cannot recall her details; only that her sensuality was like that of an artwork, an illustration for a comic book, maybe a Veronica or Betty or perhaps a Lois Lane or a pin-up girl like Grable. Nothing was real—lumber-jack in the woods with a woman companion.

The action that took place this time was a kiss, a long sensual kiss. The musty wood sent from the cabin and dark dust all around lifted that kiss to extraordinary heights. There was the unmistakable aroma of pine needles and damp musky soil; my senses raced. Unrelated thoughts of a grave sprung to mind—the burial ground of my mother; her consummated flesh festering in the corrupted mulch below, an alluring scent of frankincense and myrrh burned all around me as the perfume of decaying flowers permeated her breath. It was as though the projector of this dream borrowed elements from life and presented them as someone who has never actually experienced any sensuous moments from life; they can only relate them as one who is an observer, an observer who is trying to paint their pain. They are sharing an experience of what they hope to know, long to know, and envy.

It is an existential concept this unknown entity battles with; a painting that will never be completed so long as they daub their pain on me.

Heartbeats… we know so little of concrescence.

Kisses… Not like in the movies where every direction leads to a phony action.

My observer—the little man inside my head—and I experienced the two very different points of view. All he could witness was my hands across her back, burying my fingers in her hair. Although he and I share the same body, mind, and conscience, it is someone else that we have no control over.

My observer and I are the same; however, his dimension would not permit him to feel my emotion. Or see her face. She will not turn around for him. Something divided us… something sinister, something lifeless. A vanishing twin? One who shares a secret with someone else… It is watched over by its distant observer; sharing with a living other… observing Lydia!

Lydia's observer is haunting her. Why am I feeling this? Why are they in my brain, haunting me?

I think of that observer sometimes as a banker or loan shark dealing in miracle-giving or fate; not at all concerned with your emotional rescue, but there to judge how you might react to the passions of your soul—judging you worthy of your passions. Someone or something longing to be understood.

To be clear: Joylandia is a complicated place of the imagination. It is a convoluted television ad with layers of different messages created by media outlets to sell lifestyles; pseudo-philosophies that exploit things.

It was huge entertainment.

The people who built everything had offspring; it became engaging to watch their historical past lessons on TV without being part of it. However, we are part of it. The medium becoming the message, and the message was us—Lauren and I.

The medium is a wonderland, full of gifts. They can reap benefits from revolving door prizes of vast wealth without ever having to put skin into the game. Their religions are of peace and slow-moving harmony; they conserve nature and live very simply. They disdain from talking about toilet practices; they do realize, however, that money currency makes the world go round, and therefore, it is good to obtain it.

Garden Variety lethargic baby breeders who show up on people's doorsteps looking for a handout. Most of these folks hate the Joylandia lifestyle and everything native Joylandians hold sacred, such as sports, NASCAR racing, wrestling, and duck hunting, to name a few. But the free-for-nothing money is good, so they put up with it until their wait time is up.

I hate waiting; I have no patience. Did I mention that?

Well, well, back in the old town again.

It was an extraordinary cremation!

A nice night for a memory. To see the old city again is not without its subtle horrors.

The now-defunct Brass Nipple Foundry cast a looming shadow over the town, its chimneys wilting like stooped sunflowers that have grown too heavy for their stems.

After years of threats, concessions, and layoffs from the owners, brass was becoming too expensive and difficult to use. Constant lawsuits and pollution laws made it difficult to do business as usual. PCB fittings were becoming the rage, so Ernie and Ted Hammerschmidt, the two remaining family owners, decided to pack it up and retire.

I'll take a walk downtown. The old gin mill is still there—damn, this is creepy.

It is hard to believe this tavern still stands. A neighborhood shot-and-beer place is now the comfort zone for a few old ironworkers and a local drunk or two. Whoever took it over from Gordy and Louise had a sense of humor—the HH (Heartbreak Hotel) lounge.

It reads like a noir novel, to say the least.

Ed Ashcroft—a friendly face from the neighborhood a decade or two older—was preserved nicely from all the booze (the poor man's formaldehyde) and now a local drunk still immersed in greaser fiction with his Elvis Presley hair; passed out and loaded at the bar. His head comfortably padded in the crook of his arm, forearm at attention, and his right hand, heavily weighted with ceremonial rings of all types, was pressing into the flesh of his chubby diabetic fingers. Resting atop his duck's ass coiffed hairstyle was a pair of white aviator sunglasses that the King made famous during one of his last performances.

Outside, an old van with mounted boombox speakers was parked, blasting golden oldie hits from the fifties and sixties.

Not a bad sort Ed was; part primate, part magic Christian. On the side of the van was a hand-painted inscription that read, "Jesus Saves," featuring a metallic decal sticker of the King (Elvis, not Jesus) belting out a tune probably of Southern Baptist origin.

I remember Ed from back in the day; we partnered in shuffleboard, a game in which players push disks along a smooth hard surface into numbered scoring areas to knock down electronic pins. Partnerships were formed and the gang played for drinks—the losers would buy the winners a round. To the serious players like Ed, winning meant a free drink. He would most likely pick me as a partner since I was steady and had a pretty good bank shot. But I got bored easily and soon began slacking off. This would irritate him, causing him to stir into a coaching frenzy. He'd demand I pay more attention and concentrate on my spares. I, however, did not give that much of a fuck about it and would continue to goof around. This caused Ed great anxiety, and on second rounds, he would choose a different partner. That was fine with me; I just wanted to go back to my barstool and blend my mixed emotions over Lydia.

Ed believed that Jesus and golden oldies could save your soul.

Baptized with a jigger of scotch, he would simonize that tarnished chrome halo. Like the Silver Surfer, he coasted along the chrome shores of imagination from coast to coast where fraternities of young men sang songs of customized cars and pretty girls. With American pie, scotch, and soda, plus twenty-five cent hot dogs while cruising down the boulevard in a '56 turquoise Chevy without any dents... Poor Ed—he fucked up everything he got his hands on; just never had enough experience in anything important.

Ed snores gently like a boy in love with dreaming. And who is anyone to judge? Slow dancing toe to toe was not so bad in itself, I suppose; however, little Susie getting knocked up at 2 AM (in a town that could not imagine anyone having sex after twelve midnight) was heinous debauchery; punishable by extrication and eventual exile.

Middle-aged Elvis worshippers will forever parody the look and style of the King from a select point in time when Elvis himself was already past his prime.

You never see a young Elvis parody. With all the gilt and glamor, the beautiful slender visage and the Viva Las Vegas swagger; the billboard Valentino—*that* was the icon, the incomparable Elvis. God put beauty in the eye of the beholder, alright, and the Colonel made sure everybody looked at it.

The aging Elvis fan could never imitate a young Elvis. It will always be the bloated one in the white jumpsuit they chose to glorify.

The shot-and-beer motif is sentimental, to say the least. Poorly upholstered country-themed stools spin as a bleach blonde barmaid well over her prime swipes a frock of hair away from oversized eyelashes; she even manages to squeeze into those skinny jeans. The bartenders still polish the glasses with a sham cloth and the place smells like beer and cigarettes. One of the few juke joints left that still has a jukebox in traditional style. And for good reason, the clientele stayed the same for forty years—still has a penchant for doo-wop and golden oldie tunes. Time stopped in the nineteen fifties for Gordy and Louise and everyone else as well, especially old Ed Ashcroft.

It was a real rock 'n'- roll swing joint in the convention of the times. When Jack Koskie was five years old, his old man Gordy Koskie would put him up in one of those barstools and let him drink Cola through a straw; Momma Louise "Cline" Koskie helped Gordy keep the place up.

Running up and down the steps tending to the needs of a busy bar was a good workout for a young woman in those days. Louise kept a fine figure, and Gordy knew it, always watching and keeping keen tabs on who was fish-eyeing his wife. Louise made sure the whiskey flowed and the beer wasn't running to a flat; tapped off with just the right head was a tavern art to be respected. Louise learned everything from soup to nuts about tending bar from Gordy, a seasoned veteran behind the till. Louise was quick with a joke and never let a spill linger or a glass stay empty for too long.

Gordy and Louise ran a simple ship. A freshly painted tin ceiling and half-paneled walnut wood walls kept things classy.

Local papers kept customers aware that progress was being made every day. Time Magazine had for its cover Nikita Khrushchev as a man of the year in 1957. Iron Liege won the Kentucky Derby. And the hotties to watch were Marilyn Monroe, Jayne Mansfield, Ava Gardner, Dorothy Dandridge, Brigitte Bardot, Sophia Loren, Doris Day, Kim Novak, and Lana Turner. All graced the walls around a checkered dance floor. There were some scattered portraits of Pat Boone and Tab Hunter, but the one eye-catcher that made everyone stare was the sixteen-by-twenty-four portrait of Elvis with the button-down cowboy shirt and the red bandanna around his neck, pompadour loosely dipping to one side as a careless lock of jet-black hair perfectly crossed his forehead. And right behind him was Johnny Cash with his black shirt and white pearl buttons, smiling just enough so you know where he's been.

Any time after seven o'clock at Gordy and Louise's, folks were holding each other, moving slowly to "Butterfly" by Andy Williams or "Love Letters in the Sand," but when the Chevys pulled up, everyone knew it was "Jailhouse Rock" and "All Shook Up" they wanted to hear.

That was then. I am looking at a glossy poster for the weekend entertainment of all things. *Raja mama*, the Pakistani Elvis was going to perform.

PART TWO

"Love rules, without rules."
Italian Proverb

Ringing once, ringing twice… the phone was picked up; a man with an affected Asian dialect picked up to answer. "Hello. Lychee Nut; how can I help you?

The voice on the other end answered in a lyrical tone almost too pleasant for the usual customer on this rainy and dull Tuesday night. There was a slight trace of an accent; a British accent artificially suffused onto an Italian dialect. "Yellow, yellow, ah… dis izza Mr. Bella Chinese, the beautiful China man… Ah… Yellow, yellow can you hear me? Yellow…"

With that, the voice on the other end—proprietor and owner Xi Lee of the Lychee Nut restaurant—angrily responds. "Papaya, I know it is you. Stop calling here, or I will report you to the police."

Bella Chinese responds, "And I am sick of your rotten egg foo young. Except for the vine, no plant bears a fruit of as great importance as the olive."

"Papaya, I warn you, stop calling here. You real asshole."

The man Bella Chinese responds in a mock Chinese accent. "Xi, why you have a name like Roman Number… I call you "Eleven." Marco Polo made your noodle famous."

Infuriated Xi retorts. "You go bend spaghetti, you racist guinea…"

Bella Chinese giggles; with consummate ease, court jester on a conference call, he continues, "If the first father of the human race was lost for an apple, what would he have done for a plate of tortellini?"

"You crazy Papaya… very sick man. Go get your head examined."

Bella Chinese begins again, taunting. "Yellow… This is Mr. Bella Chinese…"

With that, the phone clicked, leaving Nazareno Papilla hanging in a void of copper wire and plastic tubing. He hung on a little longer until an analog dial tone buzzed in his ear.

He looked at the receiver then placed it back into its cradle.

Still giggling, he finished getting dressed. He applies a mousse, Brylcreem gel, to his hair and a splash of Lilac vegetal to his clean-shaven face. With admiration, he quipped, "Reno—Nazareno Papilla, you are one handsome son of a bitch."

Wiping the last bit of moisture from his fingertips, he proclaimed, joking to himself one last time, "A little dab will do ya."

He proceeded to adjusting his tie. He chose silk paisley and carefully dangled the loose end, pulling it through the loop to secure a Windsor knot—slightly old school for the times, he thought, yet retro enough to get him distinguished in the crowd. Nazareno Papilla cut a youthful figure for a man passing seventy, with just the right mix of silver to his hair, arched eyebrows, and a William Powell pencil line mustache. He was admiring his svelte physique in the hallway mirror when the doorbell rang. He peered through the side window to notice a mail carrier waiting outside with a letter and some customary mail. Making his way to the door, he greeted the mail carrier with a slight hello and casual greeting.

"What have we here?" Reno asked in dull surprise.

"I have a certified mail letter for a Mr. Nazareno Papilla. Will you sign for it?"

"I will," replied Papilla, with a sense of wonderment.

Taking the envelope from the postman, he studied it curiously before laying it down on a cluttered coffee table. It was from the law office of Wigdor, Sherman, and Strauss; it was the letter explaining the passing of a Miss Lydia Swangarden

He knew what this was; in fact, he anticipated it. All the plans were in order. Obligations met, money exchanged hands, soon the whole bizarre episode about to come to an end.

Nazareno tapped his finger against his forehead then stood still as a Buddhist monk deep in prayer. The next step—the unholy clandestine meeting with a cadaver for hire. That cagey little pervert who accepted the bribe. "I volunteered; who is to blame? Lydia? I suppose this is my price to pay; her way of making me build the cross I would be crucified on if I did not comply."

"I could walk away—walk away from it all—but then I would lose Estella. If Estella found out about Lydia, she would think me cheap and a two-bit hustler. Ha! I should care what she thinks. The *persona non grata*! Estella is no saint; scared *cercatore d'oro*! No blessing to Herbert Swangarden or myself for that matter. But I cannot help myself; I love her. I am insane for her.

When the *acetone* croaks, she will be milking me as well. We all fit so delightfully into this little puzzle—so alike all of us in our selfish deception. But Estella is the shrewdest one of all.

"I approached her thinking that I could steal her from him, thinking it a waste that a woman like that should be enslaved to a real *vecchio sciocco* for his money, never thinking she was playing me too—another well-to-do old sugar daddy to take her home when the curtain comes down for Mister Swangarden... "We Ain't Just Shag" indeed. Trite, slanted, hypocritical prophesy. I should not have led Lydia on after she found out about Estella. The betrayal of her father was bad enough, but she never suspected me. It is no wonder she is calling on my skills, asking me to soil the one talent I am proud of myself. In an appeal to my lower virtue and to carry out her vendetta—a trifecta payback on the men that have left no grace in their shadow... The father, the son, and the unholy ghost all still living, all carrying the burden of her terrible secrets and the hurt she suffered. Poor Lydia. To think of a scheme so ghastly; a hoax to be played on her—the pain she rose above.

Her skin to be flayed, dried, and shrunken, then stretched across a frame like thin leather. The ink stained into the pores like a cattle brand on the hide of oxen. Some love letters illuminated like iconography across the broad shoulders that narrowed into the small of her back; lovely gold iconic lettering in gothic calligraphy no less. She was a saint, not a martyr; although there might have been something of a sacrificial victim somewhere in her personality. I felt coolness with her at times, like another being besides her rebuking me. Something was striving within her that could drive me to death if it wanted to. A silly notion I know. But still, over all, very real.

That funeral caretaker that let me in was a repulsive creature (*l'omino disgustoso*) who presented the box to me, the pelt perfectly preserved in dry ice. It took some preparation to defrost. I was able to do my finest work once the hide was pliable again.

He worried me, this caretaker… sometimes he spoke of someone else; another inquirer. No one else knew of my deed; it was my pact with Lydia. But yet the *pazzo* little *diablo*, who perfectly removed the skin. And an excellent job at that. His patience and attention to detail led me to believe that he is no stranger to macabre perversity (the ghoulish little monster), insisting there was another visitor that day who wanted to see the tattoo. After some rejection, the mystery inquisitor left to attend the service. He never said who he was.

Forms, more forms.

Jules Wigdor
220 Constitution Court
Suite 3a
Hoboken, New Jersey

Mr. Nazareno Papilla,

My office has been instructed to deliver the contents of the attached mail to you at the request of our former client Lydia Swangarden at a timely interval after her death. It is to be delivered to and only to a Mr. Nazareno "Reno" Papilla. At this point of delivery, our obligation and all business concerning the aforementioned Lydia Swangarden are completed.

Thank you,
Jules Wigdor

It has been scarcely a week after the cremation ceremony, on the ghastly rainy day that Lydia was sent up. What could this be all about? As gruesome as it was to have finally seen that cadaver-like old man hooked up to those bubbling tubes, along with Estella by his side—the ridiculously attractive, charming young wife; a goddess, now reduced to Intra-Venus De'Milo.

Where could she have met him? At the Casino Rialto maybe, or the Flemish room—that stale soil plot that calls itself a country club; of course, Estella was no bar fly. She was very well connected to a network that she had created—genius in the making. A true sociopath, a gold digger and femme fatale to say the least. And I love her… well, for lack of a better term; I use the word loosely. I have little or no use for that word, only in mixed company or conventional settings. For me, I cannot say I have ever fully fallen in love. Let us agree, for sake of argument, that I love something about her; her obscurity, perhaps, the intrigue of her deception lures me. She is a game of chance to me—the game is played with a pistol and one bullet except she is cheating.

If she was not twisted by savage beauty and psychological sexuality (I rebuke the idea that most of her physical talents fell waste to octogenarians functioning on eighty percent imagination and fogged memory), I would have to admit I could and have unwittingly fallen into the same pond as my elderly cohorts. There is no fool like an old fool. That is a witticism I must attribute to an American sage, for the Italians might say, "I am a little trick; fool me once, fool me twice—three times the charm."

I can't say there was much mourning on her behalf. I watched her carefully; it was obvious that with the passing of Lydia—the last and only heir to the Swangarden empire—the two stepsons from the first wife Vivian completely cut off. Estella did her homework; both were useless wrecks—might even be dead. No one has been in touch for decades.

Estella stands to become the sole recipient of the old man's fortune.

I still have the business card she wrote her number on close to three years ago.

Swangarden carpets. Brilliant. She was setting herself up as Herbert Swangarden's personal secretary and eventually marrying him. "We Ain't Just Shag." Cute… That's Estella—sweet poison that burns both ends against the middle. I don't know what was in it for the old man, but I loved her—to have her there touching me with those eyes. It was too bad Lydia had to get caught up in all this—a sweet kid. The spider's web is consuming. It could have just as easily been Lydia… I just fell for Estella, that's all.

It was the night of the cremation, her little scene in the quiet room. It is nearly a decade, for Christ's sake, and she still starts right up again like a Chrysler. Poor Lydia, sweet Lydia; I led her on, I had to, I had to, I had to get to Estella somehow. It was that night Lydia, and I flew in from Texas to see her father. He was dying, or so we all thought. Lydia was by his side. She wanted to be alone with him—her father whom she had not seen for quite some time. She took his feeble hand and cradled it. Lydia's hand was like Yogi Berra's catcher's mitt.

Estella is always working, always set up. Keeps the suckers coming back like an Atlantic City card shark. I never thought of myself as a back-up plan, but I guess I was.

Estella began using the opportunities for us to be together—an excuse to get some air to clear her head led to a shameless romp at the underground parking garage. Then there was the time (she needed to be alone with her thoughts) that ended with a quickie on the porch. Each time she had to calm her nerves; the crocodile tears kept her free from arousing any suspicion. The best, however, was the separate hotel room we had secured about. a mile away called the Chateau Renaissance. It was an over-glorified motel with brash lighting and terrible lettering. The one caveat we found entertaining was that it had wall-to-wall Swangarden premier carpeting stapled all throughout it.

Enhanced loop graphics tip shear with tufted pile height-woven synthetic primary backing; the weight density was 196.608 kg/m3 and one hundred percent nylon yarn for hotel room luxury. Estella did do her homework.

Even with topical applied static protection below normal human sensitivity standard test conditions (70 degrees F.-20% R.H), we had to find a woman's hosiery store for dark taupe stockings to conceal the carpet burns on Estella's knees.

Born Nazareno Papilla in Catena, Italy

Nazareno Papilla was not one for change. He developed a type of phobia for it sometime during the war when he was forced to enlist in the Italian Army to support the cause of the fallen dictator Benito Mussolini.

He was held at attention with some infantrymen being commanded by a brute fascist sergeant that was coaching them on what to do when the Americans came over the hill. No Italian soldier in his platoon had wanted to fight the Americans. So when the Americans came over the hill and the order came to commence firing, everyone in their platoon turned their rifles on the sergeant and shot him. They threw their hands up with white flags and immediately surrendered. Nazareno looked over his shoulder at his war-torn village and what the ravages of war and insane ideology had done to the only home he had ever known. Having lost everything and everyone near to him, he could not envision himself trying to salvage a small estate of land and a house by himself. Everyone was different. Something happened to him. He realized as a seventeen-year-old boy soldier that he must give up all that was familiar to him in this old world and become a man of the new world. When he arrived in America after a short stint as a prisoner of war, Nazareno entertained himself playing cards with the Americans and learning English. He embraced change and a new culture that was before him.

The first thing he realized was that in this new land, everything was big; the bridges, cars, and signs were like nothing he had experienced in his small village Here, the sun came up over the skyline. In his village, the sun rose over a mountain range; if you stood on the top of mount Siena, for example, the side facing the sun was illuminated; if you looked back over your shoulder, the village slept in the quiet darkness of pre-dawn. His shoes did not fit properly… so he began making his own by piecing together remnants of leather from discarded shoes he had found and affixing them to makeshift soles and heels, carefully recalling the techniques shown to him by his Uncle Luciano who was a master shoemaker. Luciano was taken by the Germans to repair shoes for the troops; Nazareno never heard from him again after the war.

It was 1957 when Nazareno became fully acclimated to the United States. It would be ten years before Monte was born and almost thirty years before Lydia.

It began as an era of truth-telling. Everyone had their version. There were artists and writers and news people, underground networks of shady characters that traveled taboo circuits. You saw it everywhere in dress and hairstyle; sad songs and bubblegum, horror and romance. Lines began to blur. Social change was on the cusp. Something began to die and something was being born every day. The recipes to the new taste had bizarre ingredients, and it took some time to see the cake from between the pages of this wild cookbook; a culture that was happening. Quite like Dickens off to a new generation; all the great expectations that rolled off the presses. The new generation was restless. Something was festering beneath the surface of hometown America; the heroes were getting bored, the tough guys dying from lung cancer.

"What do you think that is?" she asked me, again
pointing with her stick, "that, where those cobwebs are?"
"I can't guess what it is, ma'am."
"It's a great cake. A bride-cake. Mine!"
(A scene from "Great Expectations")

The only novel Nazareno "Reno" Papilla would ever read from cover to cover in his lifetime was "Great Expectations."

"In this story, there is everything you need to know about life," he would often say.

It was a great cake—an old cake; a symbol of beliefs caught in continuity. A cake ordered at a time of celebration by a woman in love; a woman left at the altar, never to marry, never to see the light of day for many long years. So intense was this heartbreak that the very clock in the tower was suspended at the very moment of rejection, never to transcribe time again. The cake, what did it mean? Art represented into something you could consume. Its function was happiness—the talisman to be eaten up, hidden inside one being to manifest as the light of happiness, goodwill, and cheer.

Alas, an empty celebration?

Not so much different from the abandoned parfait tower that was left out in the rain at MacArthur Park a century later.

After all, it is a recipe, isn't it? All relationships are formulas to some degree; am I right? Let us look at the ingredients more closely. We get to know the familiar flavor.

In a romance, one must know the correct proportions of tenderness and honesty, kind words, and temperatures. There must be a great deal of patience and waiting time in between stages. If we cut corners or rush the process, we risk ruining the experience; experimentation can lead to disaster. It is a delicate combination of alchemy and passion.

Appetite comes with tasting; the baker must prepare the ingredients. When the ingredient is love, the madman must mix the batter.

How similar Nazareno was to Monte and Monte was to Pip (our hero of the novel); although the two human characters would never meet, they existed in a strange dimension that was held in perpetuity by Lydia's memories. If only those memories had the chance to introduce themselves… perhaps some of the missing pieces could be better.

Arranged by their acquaintance, some mystery cleared up. But, alas, we are doomed to muddle through appearances armed only with expectations great and small, filtered through assumptions; rarely basing anything on fact, but rather conjecture and wanton desire.

Life in America

Nazareno settled into an ominous and industrial community on the great east coast where there were many Italian Americans already. He perfected his English skills by taking some classes at night while working odd jobs during the day. The first complete message that Reno was able to read was an advertisement sign that hung in the window of an appliance store. It said, "New TV sets contain built-in circuitry that lets the user choose any of these channels—mono or stereo." He was proud to have read the sign completely sounding the words out as he was taught. However, he had no idea what the technological terms *mono* or *stereo* meant.

He occupied a small one-room flat, where he humbly rested listening to the new rock 'n' roll songs from his radio. One day, while listening to the radio, he heard an advertisement for a company out of Paris, Texas. The word "Paris" intrigued him; although he wasn't particularly fond of the country France, he felt a kinship to the European appeal in the name—a call from Europe so to speak. After all, he had been away from Italy for many years now; he is a full-fledged American citizen, entitling him to all the fantasies and advertising wisdom Madison Avenue can create to keep it faithful on the path.

The company was a leather-tanning business. They made saddles and hardware for the farmers and rodeo horses amongst other leather products. Armed only with the knowledge he had already acquired from his Uncle Luciano about processing leather, Nazareno called to mind some basic skills. Skins are salted with common marine salt to eliminate as much water as possible from the skin to avoid the natural hide degradation, then the soaking and tanning process. The hide is hide; how much different can it be? He remembered how he rolled a sheet of leather for his uncle after tanning. Grading them according to their natural features. Uncle Luciano was so impressed by the boy's good work that he bragged all over the village how young Nazareno will be a famous shoemaker one day. He will have a shop in Milan making shoes for all the big shots in Italy... maybe even Il Duce himself. Of course, all that was before the war.

He called the number for personnel provided by the ad and spoke with the person in charge of processing the hides; he was hired and set off for Texas.

Once there, he immediately became intrigued by the American West. The men were suntanned and burly, wearing ten-gallon hats; some carried guns like cowboys and everyone worked hard and ate steak every day, a luxury no Italian from a small peasant town could ever imagine. There were no small Italian delicatessens, and it became questionable if he would be able to gather ingredients for his home-cooked meals. The pasta was almost unheard of in Paris, Texas, at that time, but there were plentiful Tomatoes that came in from California, so he was soon making a sauce with available ingredients native to Texas; he could still make his soups and salads.

Being a foreigner himself, he became friends with Native American Indians more quickly than the local Texans. He was amazed at how some Native Americans were mistreated. He reasoned to himself that since they were here before the time of Columbus, they would have just as many advantages as Texans; that was not the case. He could understand the prejudice some had for him as an Italian, for after all he was a foreign man and originally was enlisted in the fascist army under Il Duce Mussolini when he was a boy, but the unfairness toward the native Americans confused him. He experienced the same uncomfortable reaction back on the east coast where there were seething Black and white issues. These things brought him unrest; he loved his fellow Americans all the same and did not want to take sides on these ugly displays of racial bickering. Although Reno's accent was usually the butt of jokes from the shopworkers, he was not treated as unfairly as some of the Native American co-workers were.

When Reno met his foreman that sunny afternoon, he was in awe, having never before seen anything like him in the east.

The foreman Ed Langtree drove a 1956 Brown Chevrolet Impala with huge longhorns custom applied to the hood. The interior was the genuine bovine hide of dark brown and white. Nazareno wore a traditional tie of silk that hung almost to his belt. Mr. Langtree wore two strings of twisted leather that had a sliding brooch across the top that drew up to the collar—a "bolo," they called it.

It took Reno a while to acclimate to the Texas way of doing things. But slowly, he caught on, and things got easier.

Life working at the leather tanning factory was hard. The leather had to be processed and stretched, and it was always hot at the plant. The smell sometimes was unbearable. But the finished product was beautiful. He especially liked making horse saddles; the size and beauty of them were amazing to him.

He was off on Saturdays and Sundays, and like most Italians, dressing for the occasional night-out was part of the experience.

It was depressing him that he could not find a distinctive pair of shoes anywhere. The town's local square had the garden variety of everything. The men mostly all dressed alike. It was the code. He had some things he had brought with him from New Jersey, but they were getting old now.

He began to notice that the shoes everyone wore were not very attractive; both men and women wore heavy clunkers for every occasion, especially to the church where the men wore their work shoes. He began taking discarded leather strips home and making boots that were in the style of the men's workwear but formally more stylish. He attached metal loops and leather bands for easy pull-on and pull-off and cut them to just above the ankle, seeing no need for a farmer or cowhand to go to church in full-length calf coverings. He made the leather thinner and more comfortable and then burnished the different grades of leather into a high polish, making them superior to any other boot or shoe available.

At first, some of the men scoffed thinking them too gentrified for a working man; however, a few of the younger men became enamored by the stylishness of them and had him make pairs for them. It wasn't long before requests came in to attach spurs and other unique stylings such as pointed toes and slightly elevated heal. Nazareno soon became the go-to guy for the most stylish boots in Paris, Texas.

It was the end of summer, a slow season with the expectation of things picking up by fall. A surprise visit from the company's owner caught Reno unprepared for the occasion.

Mister Samuel Clayton noticed Nazareno stretching some remnant leather after hours on a company lathe.

"Excuse me, sir," he asked Reno, "May I ask what you are doing? Everyone has gone home."

Nazareno was prompted with fear. He had only heard of Sam Clayton but never saw him. His reputation proceeded as being no-nonsense hard but fair. How he would react to a foreigner stretching discarded leather on his company tools during off-hours would be sure enough reason for dismissal, thought Reno. The only thing he could think of was to tell the truth.

"Sir, my name is Nazareno Papilla. I work as a leather tanner and saddle man. I am making shoes."

Sam Clayton not fully understanding the scope of this unusual man before him was curiously trying to figure him out.

"Shoes? Do you not have work shoes already?"

"Not that kind, sir; these are formal shoes."

"Is that so, Mr. ah… Papayas, is it?"

"Papilla, sir. It means (breast) in Latin."

Samuel Clayton pulled up a stool and half-sat in it, stretching one leg out across the floor. He studied Reno with a curious stare, slowly twisting at the end of an elegant handlebar mustache.

"For instance," Reno went on, in a somewhat clumsy Italian accent. "You are an important man, Mr. Clayton; a man whose clothes say a lot about him. But the shoes, no one ever considers the shoes…"

All that week after his encounter with Nazareno Papilla, Samuel Clayton was uncomfortable. One evening, he picked up the local paper and opened up to page three. He randomly scanned the headlines.

"San Francisco's garbage is planned to travel the scenic western Pacific Railroad beginning in 1971…."

"The Museum in Suva is Fiji worth a visit…"

"The women of the Canary Isles have beautiful figures; however, they have the propensity common to Mediterranean women of soon running to fat…"

He folded the paper, gently tapping it on his knee. From beyond the doorway, a sleepy figure came walking out while adjusting her robe and fluffing the collar around her neck to ward off an evening chill that was sweeping across the room.

"Sam, you are still up; is everything okay?" Sandra Clayton, his wife of 16 years, still kept a cutting figure for a woman nearing forty with a charming twang to her mid-western slight southern drawl. She took a seat across from him, resting her chin in her hands.

"I am fine, just restless." He reached over a little bored, absent-mindedly retrieving a fresh copy of Playboy magazine from the rack and flicked through the pages, stopping at an ad for men's shoes.

The Playboy publication was one popular magazine out of many Sam had purchased that day. He also acquired the most recent copies of Esquire and a popular sports rag to round out his cache—not to catch up on some reading or to relax into the literary content that lies therein but to study more deeply the men's fashion ads, shoe, and dress boots in particular.

Sam had developed a penchant in what the metropolitan man was doing, what covered his feet while he was pounding the sidewalks and visiting rumored notorious nightspots back east. Women were developing high-minded ideas; men were growing their hair long and dressing differently. The image of the high plains drifter that they have of us here in the west is portrayed as a man smoking cigarettes on a horse. The west is changing.

Current fashion was not something he had ever had much interest in. What went on beyond the realms of his little leather business never enticed him as this had. The germ of an idea that was planted in his head by this peculiar "eye-talian" fellow about a "fancy shoe style" was awakening a kind of latent interest in him.

Sam's creative desires were never quite challenged. Taking over a family business early on, it was expected that he would run things according to his father's wishes. Everything pretty much fell into place. It was easy to settle in a one-horse town and become complacent; become the big fish in a small pond schooling together once in a while with the local dust bowl aristocrats to discuss what toady politician will be put into power while telling dirty jokes over cigars and bourbon. The best women the town had to offer in those days usually baked pies, joined community groups, and raised children in the manner that was handed down to them from their mothers. No one rocked the boat; except for the occasional scandal here and there, it was a paradise, and it was so nice. All the quiet desperation and family disillusion were walled up nicely and covered with bright wallpaper.

"What do you think of these, Sandy? These are dress boots with buckles instead of laces; its pointed toes almost like Mexicana-style cowboy boots, cut at the ankles."

"What do you mean what do I think? These are fancy men's shoes—kind of city slicker. If you want my opinion—not your style, Sam."

"Oh no, not for me. I mean, do you think folks would buy 'em?"

"Maybe city people—folks around Dallas and the east and west coast. What has gotten into you, Sam? This Playboy mania thing making a cosmopolitan man out of you all of a sudden?"

"Sandra, I got this fella down at the factory—an "eye-talian". He is some kind of shoemaker from Italy. He has been making these really fine shoes. I am thinking of adding on to the business, expanding to men's footwear."

"Well, Sam, I always thought we were a leather and saddle business. Folks like us don't have any business in high fashion or anything like that. I know you, Sam; you get bored quickly, and your high flouting ideas always bring you to some new adventure. I swear you are a regular Don Quixote, always chasing after something."

"Now come on, woman, I am asking you what you think." Sam raddled some pages at her, staring down the ad, waiting for an answer.

"What do I think? I think you are nuts, just plain nuts, Sam, but I love it when you get passionate over something. Like when you were passionate over me. Are you still passionate about me, Sammy?"

"Sandra, I am talking about shoes. Come on now; I am serious. I see an opportunity here."

"And I see an opportunity here." Sandra opened her robe and exposed a see-through clingy negligée nightie. "I picked this out at the ladies'; hosiery shop in Galveston when I went to visit Kayla last week— at Hollywood Secrets. You like it? Now, why don't you put that magazine down and come to bed? I don't need any center-fold bunnies around here. They are libel to put ideas in your head."

Sam Clayton looked over Sandra in her provocative lingerie. The label flipped at the shoulder read Hollywood something or another—very different for her. He looked back to the shoe page, noticing how the ad was transmitting the same sensuality that his wife was projecting. He could not explain it, but something was happening, He felt as though he was suddenly part of the ad and Sandra (Sandy), his wife (girlfriend), was projecting —as though the man in the ad and the women behind him was suddenly him and her; there's something perverse about it, unsettling... downright sexy. Something is happening, he thought. America is changing... sex is selling.

It was a few months later when Samuel Clayton took an interest in Reno's ideas and expanded his tannery to making high-burnished leather products for dress shoes to broaden his market. Boots were becoming all the rage in the upcoming '60s America. Hippies and entertainers—from mod girls to wild game hunters—were covering their feet with the new styles.

Sam Clayton was no fool; he also knew there was a conflict heating up over in a strange place called Vietnam, and Samuel Clayton—with the help of Nazareno Papilla, the "breast from the west"—was banking on trying to get those government contracts for soldier utilities. Nazareno was promoted to styling consultant and rewarded handsomely but, never asked to become a partner. He stayed on as a consultant for about 20 years and left the firm as a well-off man.

This was around the time he met Lydia.

Some time had passed, as time always does.

Lydia was enjoying a booming career as Atlantis Obscura—the gorgeous amazon woman from New Jersey. She had defeated Baby Girl Thelma, and the rest was history. As the reigning champion of the American Women's Wrestling Association (AWWA), she was traveling to the United States to hold her title. It was not all moonlight and canoes for the new champion; life on the road was difficult. Towns across America were booking women's wrestling acts; televising was bringing it into everyone's home at 9 o'clock at night. Lydia was a star. Catfighting in the squared circle was creating a new audience. Everyone was making money.

It was spring in Paris—Paris, Texas, that is—when county fairs and rodeos were coming to town. The Paris arena was hosting for the first time a wrestling event. It was to be sponsored by the local rodeo that came through every year, a new entertainment venue that would merge nicely with local events in Paris, Texas.

Big Boss Freddie Talbot, the local music entertainment personality as well as impresario, was personally going to broadcast from ringside and hold interviews live with the wrestlers.

The billboard was striking. The Texarkana strangler Mathilda Linkletter and Phoebe Freeman Tag—team champions of the west—are challenging Atlantis Obscura and Peppermint Pouch Patty Mae for the world cup championship of the AWWA.

The arena is the gymnasium of an old grammar school that was going to be torn down but instead was being converted to an event center with the remaining rooms becoming concession stands. One of the concession rooms was where the Italian shoemaker Nazareno "Reno" Papilla had been experimenting with a kind of soft leather athletic shoe. This was a new venue for him by self-promoting at sporting events.

Lydia's bus pulled in to the Holiday Inn just outside of town; she unloaded her stuff and tried to get some rest before the big event that next night. Her feet were tired; she rubbed them down. Although she stood close to seven feet tall and was in the best physical shape of her life, her feet were tender and sensitive. Commercial brands just were not available to Atlantis Obscura. The gorgeous amazon woman from New Jersey was forced to wear men's modified military boots—not very attractive for a star of her stature. She spent a good part of her evening painting them with glue and sprinkling glitter over them. What she needed was a footwear designer that would understand her plight. She looked out her window over the flatlands and rolling tumbleweeds.

"Not anyone around here," she lamented.

He threw himself willy-nilly into his loosely made bed, reinventing wild juvenile thoughts that he left abandoned for a very long time. A man well into his fifties now so much has been left behind him, prime slices of youth, cut and sold like procured grass-fed veal at the farmers' market. Outside, a new generation of teenagers pounded the street—post-war baby boomers with hopes and dreams. They have only known a world free of war; free to take advantage of advertising the most innocuous form of propaganda.

Nazareno had been away from the city for twenty odd years—long enough to have developed a Texan drawl. He kept a sharp little bungalow off the edge of town, not far from the tanning factory. He drove a pale blue dodge with a white interior. He wore a Panama-style Stetson and a bolo tie, creased dungarees with a white shirt, and snakeskin shoes. Not leather. He was sick of leather. He bought them in Dallas while on a business trip from a man who made shoes and strange-looking clothes out of snakeskin. Nazareno needed a change—he needed a wife; he needed a life.

Nazareno was drinking tequila with his friend of many years—Heve (pronounced He-vary with the accentuation on the long A), which was his nickname; his real name was Hevataneo. Their friendship that had developed from the early years. They became friends when one day Heve came to his bungalow with a bag of cornmeal. Reno cooked some polenta, and they drank tequila and beer, listening to pop music on the radio. While drunk, they got onto the topic of the origin of names.

Reno stood up and said with some exaggerated bravado, "I am Nazareno Papilla, Nazareno being "the man of Nazareth" and Papilla "being a female breast"; you know—the "teat," so I suppose I am a savior and a tit."

Vat—that is what everyone called Heve—looked up at him with an expressionless face. He thought for a while and then responded.

"I suppose that in your culture that has some great significance. It does not mean anything to me. I can make no sense of it since I am neither Christian nor female. I think more of a cow than a woman when I hear the word "teat." No offense—my religion involves animals more than people. It is proper that I deem the burro sacred."

The Nazarene held up his glass, and they toasted.

"Your name, Hevataneo—does it mean anything? The Nazarene leaned back and pulled a cold beer from a cooler he took a deep slug to wash down the burning tequila.

"My whole name is Hevataneo—it is Cheyenne; it means hairy rope."

The conversation went pretty much along those lines for the rest of the evening until Heve said he had to go. Reno wrapped up some polenta and offered it to Heve. "Here, take this back to your children. Children in Italy love this—add sugar or honey."

"Thank you," replied Heve. "It is amazing that your country, Italy, is so far away and yet they know what cornmeal is."

"Not so amazing, my friend; I think Columbus brought corn back from his voyage."

"You mean the Indians gave him the corn and then he brought it back to Italy and now you eat it here and give it back to me?"

"Something like that."

"That is the circle of life," harrowed Heve.

"Does that mean anything to the Cheyenne?" Reno replied quizzically.

"Fuck if I know…"

And so it went.

In a night of half-dazed dream sleep, the Nazarene was young again; a youthful lad of Italy running amongst the orchards, chasing Carmella the "sweet apple" and finding her hiding always in the most secluded spot, always dressed in her plain gingham style dress, an apron girded on her hips to nest apples and chestnuts that grew wild along the road. "Her shoulders broad and tan smooth and glistening like caramel, bolstering a generous cleavage rounding out the front as she leaned forward to gather her apples from the road; always aware, sneaky, and obvious at the same time, checking my reaction to her subtle flirtations; testing me always to see how much I knew, if I would take the bait," he chided himself.

"Then one afternoon, in heated frustration, we fell to the earth behind an abandoned shed in mid-country. She made us a cot of straw and blankets. As she reclined, some straw attached itself to her hair in such a way it appeared as though she was wearing a golden tiara. Her body was firm and pliant. A droplet of perspiration beaded beneath the fold of her breasts; her pubis sweet coriander and musk. Heat radiated from her in waves pulsating a natural burn. She was always so much cleverer... always three steps ahead... I am sure she outwitted the Germans," he whispered in half-delirium. "Oh, my sweet apple, how I miss thee."

One of his favorite movies was Doctor Zhivago—not for any war elements but purely for the love story. The part where Yuri was on the bus and thought he recognized Lara walking along the avenue. How Yuri was overwhelmed with the idea of seeing his beloved Lara again after all the conflict and unrest. To speak with her once more and discuss only things they would know; sharing synchronized thoughts and experiences that no one else in the world would understand. How he died on the cold street alone—so close. It reminded him of Carmella. The war—one day I will return to Italy and try to find Carmella. Nazareno was always making proclamations to himself. In moments of loneliness and isolation, he would call out to that which was familiar to him; things from the past because he never considered time as exiting in the future—or the present for that matter. For Nazareno "Reno" Papilla, there is only the past.

"When it comes to bed, there is no difference between a poet, a priest, or a communist," he quoted. After mumbling a prayer in broken English, he fell off to sleep.

Upon awakening, some new sensation was afflicting his senses. Something strange and wonderful had happened to the Nazarene. A new impression emitted from his amygdala flooding his being with a new desire. For the first time, he heard the name "Paris" the way born=and=bred Americans might be affected by it—as something to be aroused by and looked into. He was beginning to feel the attraction and romanticism natural Americans had for foreign countries—the mystique they craved.

He was inundated and infused with fantasy, completely out of character for a man like himself. Not being born in America with all its glitzy glamour, its isolation, the superficial culture changes—cars getting bigger, side streets getting smaller. Girls in mod dress then suddenly more conservative. The radio brought news; the television put faces on it… adding color to the screen-projected emotion, making the characters more real; everyone could be a star. It was difficult for him to see the overseas continents as anything more than recovering nations ravaged by war, where everything was broken and nothing ran on time.

At once, there was a relief from a structured mindset; artists and cabaret dancers poured onto the cobblestone streets from smoky saloons and along the left bank was Pinot noir. It was Palisades Park, New Jersey; along the seine, a new confusion tore at him. He questioned himself.

"All this is fine for an inquisitive romantic American, but I— Nazareno "Reno" Papilla—I was almost shot in the ass, for Christ's sake."

When Lydia first entered the shop to inquire about handmade athletic shoes, Reno did not know what to make of her. She was looking around snapping her gum and finally decided on a style she was comfortable with. She turned to Reno and asked.

"Hi, can I have a pair of athletic shoes made in the style of those on that shelf over there? My name is Atlantis Obscura…" She laughed a zestful laugh as she explained, "I am with the wrestling foundation—perhaps you've heard of me? A girl just can't find the right shoes anywhere these days."

Reno looked at her. Reno, well over six foot himself, still had to look up to take her all in. He led her over to the fitting area where he took her measurements. The first thing he thought was, "The sexual frustration I feel seeing all those bare toes—all soft, smooth, and painted with pretty colors—is overwhelming. It always seems to bring to mind the adage, 'Water, water everywhere, but not a drop to drink.'"

The day was a beauty, an absolute scorcher—sixty-five degrees and not a cloud in the sky. The Nazarene was buzzing with sexual arousal at the mere thought of ogling her cabriole leg a well-conditioned calve with the knee curving outward and the ankle curving inward, posing a sensual bend that leveled out into an ornamental foot. She was fine; a geometric-like furniture. So he got straight down to business, focused on the matter at hand, and before he knew it, she said, "Call me Lydia, I am at that hotel behind the Arena..."

"Oh, the Marquis?"

"Yes, that's the one. I can never remember those French names..."

Reno begins his affair with Lydia—the female wrestler that needed a new pair of shores.

Vlad.

It was his day of rest. Every Sunday, Vlad woke up early and began his time together with the Lord by breaking the bread of a deli bagel and washing it down with a steaming cup of coffee. This ritual was one of the few observances he still enjoyed. Having found no fault or disillusionment in it, this harmless practice was one that somehow brought him closer to godliness.

Having tended so long to the miserable and wretched, many of the strong beliefs he had instilled in him by his Jesuit brothers had faded over the years. The manifestation of miracles in small everyday occurrences made more sense to him now than all supernatural phenomena he studied his whole life.

The age of miracles has passed. However, every day withstanding could be considered to produce amazing life-changing effects if one was to follow the rules or simply; just let things go.

There seemed to be no real miracle for the insane; stillbirths and the aborted stand no chance on their own to reach out in prayer for forgiveness of their original sin.

He looked around sipping his coffee and strolled over to the window where the morning light was busting through just bright enough to provide enough light to read the paper without putting the lights on.

The window view from his room transformed a dingy city park into a grid of tiny gardens and ponds.

Here, one particular shady dogwood tree was coming into bloom. Birds nestled around its branches, welcoming the soft newly formed buds with gentle pecks and kisses. There were instances when the stillness and calm of nature brought together the order of things; an unspoken truce between the chaos that man wrought and the ebb and flow that make up a day.

He looked down onto a magazine half-buried under some bills and paperwork. A portion of the exposed cover revealed an illuminated reproduction of J.M.W. Turners' "The Golden Bough," the painting aglow of imagination surrounding the little lake of Nemi—"Diana's mirror," as the ancients knew it to be.

Vlad reflected daily on the mythology he studied back at the Jesuit college oh-so-many years ago. And before that, and before that, and before that, he had the long hand of ancient wisdom scripted across a papyrus leaf recording the folly of man and his gods. Intrigued was he of how similar it still is, changing only the names to protect the innocent while dreaming. "Sleep, my child; close your eyes so you don't feel it when I send a barbarian into your village to drive a stake through your heart and slaughter thy young," the gods would whisper.

Lydia could haunt these ancient woodlands; she could be at home sequestered with goddesses to love and be forsaken all in vain for the amusement of the deities.

One could not help thinking after hearing Monte's tale that she was a rare and beautiful "everyday goddess" as she was. Her virtues and vulnerabilities read like a want ad across the Olympian newsprint for all the gods to muse.

> AVAILABLE:
> Good-looking goddess of no particular deity;
> A big girl.
> Jane of all trades.

My one godly virtue: I will continue to grow as long
as you entertain me.
Always hip, always mod, always cool.
I am seeking a deity who is not ashamed to grow
with me.
I will rock your world.
Cupid does not apply;
I could eat you for breakfast.
Just saying.

These are not times for dreaming. "How disturbed we are,"
Vlad considered.

A woman whose only fault, for the most part, was that she could
not stop growing. It was almost supernatural in its manifestation; the
more she consumed in life, the more she grew, expanding like the
universe but never filling up.

Monte was right about one thing—the astrological connection
they seemed to share. It was modern-day mythology—the expansion
of time and space to increase the stature of the hero; the remarkable
elastic of placement of events in such a short period spent together.
As in a myth, there is no calendar; events leap from a dream sequence
across the sky and incinerate as they get closer to the sun.

The almighty godhead pulls the man into the crucible—a
mortal witness to the flesh of frail persons of what someone can and
cannot endure.

In Monte's case, it is the frail nature of his soul.

"How magnificently brilliant we have become, and yet we
cannot let go of godlike urges to play like children—gambling the
stars and eternity for beauty and immortality."

How peaceful and rolling eternity would be, if not for man
confounding it with mortal attachments; encoded in the very nucleus
of passion is the framework to subjugate.

Nevertheless, it is much more rewarding for Vlad, as a confidant
and life coach, to appreciate Monte's romantic achievement in the
light of defiance against convention and limitation. He can only be
doomed for tragedy—the sweet pain of wanting something you can
never have. And perhaps that is it.

Vlad put on his pants, a clean shirt, and a cloth coat. He stepped outside and strolled along the meandering walkway past benches and the smoky cans; some of the homeless burned leaves in metal trash barrels overnight to generate extra warmth. The walk was a short one to the pond.

Two long island geese nestled by a clump of the plant like grass. "My private swan garden," he thought to himself.

He thought for a moment of Lydia, and the transformation thereof.

A poem came to mind fitting to our modern-day heroine Lydia.

The poem "Leda and the Swan" was more of a sonnet—very beautiful. It has our Lydia behind it confused by transformation.

The designation is at once extremely significant. This is the case of "Leda and the Swan." The title is an allusion to the story of Leda—a princess denying advances from Zeus.

Zeus, so taken by Leda's beauty, would not be turned away and transforms himself into a swan.

When Zeus appears on the lake as a swan, he is embraced by Leda, thinking that this new swan so magnificent and beautiful is a gift from the gods for her pleasure; once embraced, however, she is raped by Zeus and becomes pregnant. She is also pregnant from her husband King Tyndareus and therefore is baring four children in her womb. Two sets of twins.

Vlad took a notebook from his pocket and jotted down some notes.

"Ironically," Vlad wrote, "the idea of rape in mythology was not quite what it means today... rape in mythology was understood as rapture; likened more to falling in love—a closeness to be shared with angels more so than the violent rage we think of it today. An overcoming passion, so to speak, much closer to the emotion of capricious fancy rather than to any emotional disturbance we would call to mind in our present time." Vlad pauses in thought. "At least— which is how I would like to think of it—in the case of our Lydia, of whom I am drawing a parallel case to Leda; again, I must admit I am growing a morbid fondness for Lydia… There is something alive still dwelling in her; something separate that can ensnare.

Lydia, a twin…

Having only known her through the webs and murky undertones of Monte's dossier of her—a love-hate description, to say the least—I can't help thinking there is more."

"Am I becoming infatuated with a ghost?" Vlad wondered.

"Yeats is very descriptive in this sonnet:

her thighs, "the dark webs," the sensual rape occurring; Leda attempting to push the swan's "feathered glory" from her "loosening thighs", but is unsuccessful. Feeling strange and removed, I feel myself succumbing to the "strange heart beating". "A sudden blow: the great wings beating still -Above the staggering girl, her thighs caressed by the dark webs, her nape caught in his bill,"

Yeats continues in this manner until the last line of the poem stating; "Before the indifferent beak could let her drop?" It is Lydia that is lying under all the white rush and feels the heart beating of the swan. "…oh, did I say Lydia?"

> Lydia, oh, Lydia
> Say, have you met Lydia?
> And so enters Groucho Marx dancing across the floor
> with a cigar pointing upward.
> A group of chorus girls in sequence costumes dancing
> around him.
> Come along and see Buffalo Bill with his lasso
> Just a little classic by Mendel Picasso
> Here is Captain Spaulding exploring the Amazon
> Here's Godiva but with her pajamas on
> I said Lydia (He said, Lydia)
> They said Lydia (We said, Lydia)
> La La!

And what do I know of our Lydia? Yes, there was something that happened in her past concerning the estranged stepbrothers. That shall remain a mystery.

I have taken it upon myself to launch a private investigation into her past, not on any account of Monte—he knows nothing of my venture—but of my own free will and overzealous curiosity; I want to know more about her. What harm could it do? It could, for the most part, bring some insight into my therapy for Monte.

So, with some investigation, I have found that Lydia's natural mother had died giving birth. A medical report completed at the time from Harborside Medical, Anaheim, California, pronounced a stillborn breach and death by hemorrhage of one Natalie Swangarden, Lydia's natural mother.

This might explain something.

Lydia might have suffered a form of survivor's guilt that led to her determined antics, her over achievement behavior, her constant running away. Having seen the graves of both her mother and twin sister most likely numerous times, it is not unlikely that she might have suffered some deep remorse about her mother and sister dying, and she left to take on the world illegitimately.

Who would know for sure? I have never met her nor ever will. Only Monte might have some insight or clues… However, I am counseling him, not her.

In his life, Lydia played such a small part; a few precious summers still the impact of her personality haunts him. The chemistry of those two was poisonous. Completely mismatched, destined to fail from the get-go. Yet they longed for each other. In a sin, a sinister separate way, as if there was another actor from that womb…

I think somewhat mysteriously, outside the norms of what my practice teaches, there might be more. Lydia, big like Texas, Monte says. Could she have been living for two? Through some supernatural transcendence; could Lydia have been possessed by her dead sister? They were to be twins. Perhaps they feel like one together? Is it possible the souls had stayed intact although the flesh was separated at birth, Lydia growing in size to double her dimension?

"I am a man of science; I should not be reasoning this way."

"I should not be developing an attachment to a ghost."

A vanishing twin.

Lydia…

I had in my life lost my siblings, but not separated at birth. I have no real memory of them. I feel no true sense of loss that I can relate to. The horror of what happened in that village as I burned with a fever that winter. What right have I to have lived? I feel the guilt also. It was a fever that could have and should have killed me. If not for the fate of some wondering Jesuits looking through the rumble and stumbling onto my suffocating body, my demise would have completed the genocide executed unto my family by those barbarians.

How lonely Lydia must have been, carrying around so many secrets; living for two—soulmates sharing one life? A mysterious unknown other looking out, another entity looking in—never complete; even Monte tore apart by the dualism.

What do I tell him? I doubt that he knows any more than what he has told me.

I feel this constant tugging at me from… from Lydia. But is it Lydia, or the other? Are the souls of all lost children together in one place that they can reach out and tug at us—we the survivors. Lydia's twin is pounding at the portal for release, forever witnessing through a glass womb. I am not married. Lydia has never married. I want to save Monte, and so did she. I can now sense what she was living through—living for a dead sibling. It could have been the other way around, but it wasn't.

I stand here now looking out at two swans circling the pond. Swans mate for life. If one should die, the other might not be able to carry on. Is Monte going to die? The sibling can never live, but the survivors can die. I fear Monte's death to be the only genuine outcome.

Monte is being driven mad by the desire and envy of a jealous sibling that is living through Lydia. Angry and frustrated, it will not turn back… still pounding the glass womb for its freedom. Although Lydia has given up the ghost for Monte some three decades ago, the jealous sibling has not. Living through Lydia, it could still pursue Monte; with Lydia dead, Monte must die also if they are to be together. My God! This demon fetus might be driving Monte to suicide so they can all be together.

And the muse arrived very beautifully and singing.
So can I say that our love is legendary?
I must say, I do not feel it when I am alone in a hotel
lobby
With a bottle of cheap Champaign and a plate of
deviled eggs.
We, with a view from the bridge,
All about you and techniques
The Odyssey sequel
He returned home again, the same as the first time.
May God grant that you go from my side quickly
To put yourself back in the Cathedral.

Back at the apartment, Vlad sat at his desk and fiddled through a box of papers and random junk. He pulled out a calendar from a few years back, old and faded; it was given to him by the priest during a Christmas party. He saved it because each month was represented by a saint. It was there on the 11th month of the year when he found what was familiar to him—one more missing piece in this cosmic circle.

It was an iconic photo of a saint. The golden framework and gilded lettering set on top of a black background. Here is what the harbinger of things to come pronounced.

Saint Hugh of Lincoln is the patron saint of swans. His feast day is on the 17th of November. Saint Hugh of Lincoln is also the patron saint of sick children.

Hugh of Lincoln was born in 1135 in Avalon, France. He died in London, England, in the year 1200.

Hugh's mother died when he was only eight years old. His father was Lord William of Avalon. Hugh got his education at the convent of Villard-Benoit. He became a deacon at the age of 19 and was appointed prior of the monastery at Saint-Maxim.

In 1160, Hugh joined the strict order of Carthusians in the Grande Chartreuse. The Carthusians spent most of their time in solitude and prayer. Hugh became a procurator in 1175.

Hugh was highly respected. He was a people-person. His good reputation was rumored far and wide.

King Henry II of England heard about this extraordinary man and requested he come to England to be the prior at the newly founded Charterhouse at Witham in Somerset. Henry II had founded Charterhouse to make penance for murdering Saint Thomas Becket.

In England, Hugh often used his wit, charm, and strong sense of humor to calm the king when the king had his angry fits. Hugh was deeply loved by so many. He made people feel calm and at ease, especially children. In 1186, he was appointed the bishop of Lincoln.

He was known to be unafraid, defending those who were discriminated against. There are stories about how he, unarmed, challenged an angry mob that was prosecuting innocent Jews. He defended the Jews and, thanks to him, the rioting mob set the captured Jews free.

Saint Hugh of Lincoln was widely known for his unusual friendship with a swan. Hugh and his swan were best friends. The swan followed him about everywhere he went on in his estate. The swan ate from his hand and slept in his bedroom.

The swan stayed loyally by Hugh's side until Hugh died in 1200. Reports say that the swan was by Hugh's bedside when he died.

Naturally, Hugh's emblem is his beloved swan.

In a Redemption Army salvage boutique over a shelf piled with souvenir cups, tarnished cuff links, and assorted bric-a-brac, there hangs a pair of leather dance shoes. The shape is plain, rounded at the toe, carefully curved at the heel; the sole a rich and complex composition of woods to bend and endure. A lace-up surrounds the ankle of the softest leathers with stares embroidered along the edge to project popularity and championship persona.

When they were purchased by Rainy Clause—a freelance set designer and post-flower-child living on St. Mark's Place right up the street of Trash and Vaudeville, a popular boutique where she was doing a window display—no one had a clue as to where these shoes could have come from or what could have prompted its creator to make a shoe so ornate and aesthetically pleasing in a size that was so brazenly bizarre.

The girls at the counter stood around as Rainy unveiled them to the staff.

"Amazing!" was one reaction.

"My God, they are enormous. They are so feminine and beautiful… but for a woman? Too carefully handcrafted to be wasted for a prop of any kind," replied Rainy.

This is the mystique and fun part of boutique buying; the history that lies behind the object. An old ring or a solemn and well-preserved personal accessory; pocket knives and ties—who could have abandoned these personal treasures kept alive for a lifetime and now most likely to be discarded at a person's demise?

The mystery that is as old as the pyramids. You think they belonged to a big transvestite or someone like that—strange, but whatever; they somehow made their way to the redemption shop. *I suppose I can put flowers in them or something*, Rainy thought.

So is the story of Lydia's shoes. One day, they found their way to a recycling bin shortly after her trunk and suitcases were removed from the carter hotel. She was pronounced dead from a heart seizure on that brisk and gloaming evening in Paris, Texas.

She had written a will—more like a request on behalf of her attorneys to have some demands attended to after her death. There was no one left in her life. She had only to live in the past; there was no future for her in those later years.

The requests were simple. Her bills and all outstanding debts are to be paid from the remaining cash in her account, which was ample due to a trust fund that she never abused. Her clothes and any remaining things of value were to be donated to the redemption army salvage in NYC. And last but not least—her love letters were to be sent to "Monte" at Chevalier Sons of the Liberty Boarding House, Bayonne, NJ.

All the details had been carefully worked out. Even Monte's address was sought out by a diligent agency.

Upon death, the body would be sent to the funeral home where a certain undertaker, JH, would perform the service—removing the part of her skin where a tattoo was carefully laid out in cursive lettering, inscribing what could only be described as a series of love letters. These are messages of an intense feeling of tender affection and compassion. These are personal messages to an unknown recipient held in secret and private by the deceased and the attorney representing this case.

Post note addendum:

The procedure should be done at the time before or immediately after autopsy to preserve the integrity of the skin. It would be picked up at said disclosed location by N. Papilla and then dried and shrunken into 8"x10' letter form. N. Papilla has agreed to these conditions and will oversee its execution; in return, he will be exonerated from all ties, past and present, concerning Lydia Swangarden and any members of her family, living or dead. And all truths and incriminations that may fall on N. Papilla and his affairs concerning the Swangardens are dissolved and exonerated by this last will and testament.

- Jules Wigdor, attorney for the
estate of Lydia Swangarden

A note from Lydia Swangarden: *If Nazareno "Reno" Papilla defaults on any of his obligations or tries to weasel out in any way, he will be confronted by the investigation agency handling this case, and all his discretions will be held against him and those involved.*

Lydia.

It was a balmy evening. Sticky dew-like droplets hung on everything. Xi Lee stepped out onto the garden behind the Lychee nut restaurant and walked over to the saga palm he had been observing.

It was wilting and top-heavy for the pot it was in. Xi had plans to transfer it to a larger pot but was putting it off for some time now. He was becoming more sentimental these days, and on misty evenings and early mornings, he enjoyed quiet meditation with his plants that he would refer to as his children. He observed the ceramic container and the crack that ran through it; how the soil and roots of the palm melded together, keeping the oriental jar from slitting completely in half. Out of respect for the integrity of the ceramic, he was reluctant to make the change.

Old age was driving his decisions more frequently these days; although still in good health, the spontaneity of tending to his beloved garden was yielding to the pleasure he took in just watching them bend and sway to the urban breezes rolling down and around from the alleyways and rooftops.

This particular morning, Xi had a peculiar feeling of unrest; a foreboding nostalgia and aloneness. He looked on to the painted pottery, an artist's depiction of his childhood homeland. In quiet meditation—his way when he was alone with his thoughts—he began piecing together a story that was as old as man himself.

The one pot in particular that he focused on told a story. A common design—the message has been taken for centuries but continues to repeat just the same; this time, however, in fragmented willow pattern.

The rebus symbols in cobalt blue and white told a tale of star-crossed lovers; a wealthy Chinese man's daughter and her father's lowly accounting assistant. When the father discovers their love, he fires the assistant and builds a fence around his property to keep him away. *You'll always see a fence around the teahouse*, he thought to himself.

The boat in the pattern carries a rich duke, who arrives with a chest of jewels and plans to marry the girl. The lover sneaks in and steals the jewels and the girl. The couple runs across the bridge to escape to an island, but the father is close behind with whip in hand. The couple is killed. The gods, taking pity on the lovers, allow their souls to take the shape of doves and fly off together.

"The gods in these ancient stories performed miracles frequently."

"It seems we mortals can never get out of our way."

"Where did my people with all their hard luck and misery ever conceive the notion that something outside themselves would save them? We are not thought of as romantic people by most Westerners. However, love produces desperation wherever it lays its head."

Nonchalantly, Xi passes a hand over his plants. Bowing ceremoniously, he sits on a bamboo chair, observing his open garden.

"They will outlive me—these palms," he whispered to himself. "If only they could care for me as I care for them. One day, they will miss me when I am gone."

His friend, Nazareno, gave the plant that inspired him on this balmy evening some years ago when he first opened the new location for the Lychee Nut.

Only twice did he have to relocate since the Lychee Nut's opening; once over a rent issue and a second time for the need of a larger kitchen.

It was on a crepuscular evening, such as this, some thirty-odd years ago. He and Nazareno became friends—two foreign men trying to work out the details and entanglements of being reborn and resurrected; finding themselves alone in a city that was holding a flame to one of the greatest melting pots this side of the Hudson River.

The Nazarene—Mr. Bella Chinese—handed over the plant to Xi and said, "Tonight, the immigrant son of Italy and a China man was chosen to live here at an hour when I huddle over my lunch pail."

Xi smiled to himself in revere.

"What a confused idiot this Breast of Nazareth is; he cannot even express himself properly."

Xi looked down toward his foot and contemplated *its* design—a deformed casualty drooping from his pants leg.

When Xi was a young man in China his foot was mangled in a machine press at a factory where he was working. The press was antiquated and timeworn. Its function was to separate fabric threads for garments. The machine was altogether clumsy and awkward to use. Work was hard and burdensome.

Xi was feeding raw cotton into the chamber when he suddenly lost his balance, falling forward into the gears and twisting his foot.

The medical assistance in China—being what it was at that time—produced botched operations and poor facilities, causing him to lose a few inches in his left leg and disfiguring his foot and calf.

Unable to continue work at the factory, he took on as a cook in a Chinese soup kitchen and soon realized he had an inbred talent for food preparation. He eventually brought his skills to America where he was able to continue working as a line cook until he opened his shop—the Lychee Nut. Having found his niche, he lived happily ever after.

"There aren't that many Chinese people who want to leave China for good these days," Xi pondered to himself, thinking how different things were for him and the new generation of kinfolk he encounters some 60 years later. "A lot may say they want to leave China —usually to move to America or somewhere—but these people generally have no idea what moving out of their culture implies…"

Lots of Chinese people Xi has gotten to be friends with over the years have different attitudes about migrating; some are strictly modern and some just want change. He knew some who have been to America, returning to their homeland in revelation at how uncomfortable they were in a fantastical land that, according to their underground news, is a paradise.

Once they realize the inconvenience of traveling everywhere by car, try the awful American Chinese food, and realize that most Americans have never heard of their favorite dishes, they soon realize how distant the two countries are from each other in both miles and cultures. The great mosaic has much to add to its tapestry, missing the point that America is a culture that morphs by osmosis; it changes on a neighborhood level more so than being frozen to an established status quo. The trend is constantly changing, given to the diverse demographics of its society.

The experience of not being able to get an Eastern remedy for a common cold or to be served ice in their drink during the dead of winter are only small inconveniences; speed bumps on the road to acclamation. One soon realizes that you have the freedom to accept the ice or not; you might even have a completely new suggestion as to how your beverage might be served—all options would most likely be considered. However, plenty of Chinese people are happy to remain in China where they are most comfortable.

Immigrants from anywhere experience trials and errors. Change is strange, to say the least, but the result is that not everyone who tries their hand at living abroad will want to stay there forever or even for the long term.

Not so with Xi, who saw himself as an Asian Odysseus. How he struggled with mythology in those days until he was proud of his English enough to place a bruised and battered copy of Homer's Odyssey beside his worn and tattered volume of Lao-tzu. So proud was he to have mastered it; he even read the version from James Joyce.

His uneven foot was always a problem; as the weeks and months went by, the constant standing and shifting of weight, compounded with kitchen demands, brought much discomfort and stress. Orthopedics was expensive, and he was a foreign man immersed in old-fashioned ways.

One day, a stranger of unusual character came into the Lychee Nut. He was tall with a broken American accent and a pencil-thin mustache—handsome in a movie star sort of way; he sat down and ordered pork fried rice and lemon chicken.

Xi prepared the meal and brought it to the gentleman's table. Xi could tell he was a different kind of person—a little eccentric maybe, with a strange sense of humor; for instance, he unfolded his napkin strangely, fumbling with it in a wave of tosses and doublings that might remind one of a magician about to pull a bouquet of daisies from underneath. He was captivating the small crowd with his unusual movements.

Xi, always conscious of how an American would react to a situation, stepped beside him for a moment to contemplate how, for example, might an American observer be moved to show disappointment when a flower or dove does not appear from beneath the serviette.

Xi was worried his fickle customers would blame the establishment for a disappointing floorshow.

Xi thought to himself, "It is American to be entertained by others' silliness and embarrassment; this is humor, if one is to believe what one sees on the television. This stranger better have a trick up his sleeve."

The stranger introduces himself right away. "Hello."

"Yes, hello, sir." Xi answered, nodding.

"I am Mr. Bella Chinese, the beautiful China man."

"Yes, is that so? I am Xi, I am Chinese also…"

The stranger looked at Xi's feet and said, "Your shoes are not fitting properly."

"I know, I have a problem with my foot."

"I make shoes. My Uncle from Italy taught me how I can fix your shoes for you. May I look at your feet?"

"Sir, are you not worried that your meal will get cold? Perhaps another time?"

Xi was becoming uncomfortable with the stranger's oddness; he was hoping this was not going to be a problem.

"It is only rice, and the chicken will not fly away." The stranger was charming. "It will only take a minute to get your measurements; here put your foot on this chair, and let me look."

"Sir, my customers might find this strange."

The stranger went on in his persistent way, "It will only take a moment; I have already sized you up in my head,"

Xi stood with one leg hoisted, much to the amazement of the sparse crowd completely attentive to the stranger; Xi did what he was told as though he were a patient at the doctor's office.

The stranger removed from his pocket a tape measure and began measuring Xi's shoe—length, width, and most importantly, depth, figuring he would need to add on about two or three inches of needed rubber sole and heel support. Xi could not believe he was allowing himself to be manipulated by this man to such a degree; however, he was helpless against his charisma.

Smiling and somewhat bursting with embarrassment, Xi addressed his customers, quite wittingly feigning a pseudo-Chinese inflection. "Him shoe repairman; he makes my foot even."

The most American patrons eyed their alien neighbors with a sideward glance of glee. Some looked on kindly with sympathy, smiling back and nodding; others giggled; the stranger worked on as if no one else was in the room involved in his measuring, once again performing a magic trick that had no immediate prestidigitation.

"There! I have everything I need; I will bring the shoes back to you soon."

In a second, everything went back to normal; the stranger attended his plate as the customers went about their dinners as though the whole situation had not taken place.

When the stranger returned in a few days, he presented Xi with a pair of magic shoes. Xi's new shoes were round and roomy with the left sole three inches thicker than the right, carefully crafted and contoured to compensate for the curvature of the instep and upper surface of the damaged area.

It was the beginning of a wonderful friendship for a long time to come. However, Nazareno, for reasons no one would ever quite understand, always would refer to himself as Mr. Bella Chinese. Xi was always entertained by this, and on more than one occasion, he would feign awkward martial arts movements, bow with hands clasped in courtesy, and repeat in a tone worthy of a Shaolin priest, "You must always keep the name Bella Chinese, you know."

The Nazarene

What can make a legend? In everyone's life, there is a story. In every life, there is death. Between the pages of this scant novella, there is a beginning middle and an end. How similar life's journey is too great art in that, peering between the lines, shapes, colors, forms, and images emerge from the scene of a great drama—proof and fact that someone has been there; a slaughter, the life and death of a single moment, the compound interest on a dime.

So, what of legend? The secrets change hands in a boardinghouse lobby.

No one expects to win because they have already failed.

What is left is the stillness, the light on inanimate objects; the turpitude of one's thoughts.

Can the passage be measured in miles, road markers, highway signs?

What is love, lost to the foolhardy that it should be deemed legendaria—fabulous, epic, fantastic, *maravilloso*, infamous?

Maybe so.

There remains the most important act in the ritual.

The actor speaks, listens, or is silent.

There are no shrieks, no shouting, no groans of remorse; just the formal dignity of tragedy—the kind that befalls a man when he is beaten from the start but continues with the game to its ill-fated end.

Hotel by a railroad station.

Western motel—awful interior; green, beige, a tepid shade of cadmium reds.

Under a burning sun;

An empty room;

Sunlight on brownstones, giving way to more emotional color strokes;

Dabbed in linseed oil and turpentine;

An Edward Hopper painting is what you have when an Estella is through with you.

Elastic isolation that surrounds everything—it expands and contracts like a universal heartbeat.

Legend brings with it some history. Far from being a magnificent background for the tragic, there is always a smidgeon of personal passion in the most intricate relationships.

The glorified self is now a measuring rod used to check the height, width, and length of each shadow on the wall.

Nazareno Papilla—the Nazarene, the breast of life—deplores the fact that his old age seems limited to outdated modes of thinking compared to Estella who is still young and now quite wealthy after the passing of old man Swangarden who died of natural causes one fine afternoon, a day as good as any other, alone in his lovely home while Estella was shopping with a young man she met on a train.

The obituary was a disparate collection of words to be read by no one. Estella pieced it together herself. A concise paragraph that explained the *who, what, when,* and *where.*

A few former business associates responded with condolences, although no one showed up at the funeral service.

Old man Swangarden had sold the business a few years back, washing his hands of the whole thing; retiring to a few cozy last years spent passing gas into the crushed velvet cushion of his favorite easy chair while being attended to by his doting young trophy Estella.

She waited on him hand and foot and handled his affairs up until he gasped his last breath, then, with preparations made in advance, she whisked him off to the crematorium.

When the family attorney informed her that she was the sole heir, she could not restrain her tears; full mourning lasted a full week and consisted of clothing made of dull black fabrics without embellishment or jewelry. She wore a veil to cover her face when she left the house. She avoided invitations and frivolous events during that time. The veil was Chanel. The dark dress and shoes exceeded fifteen thousand dollars. Her tailor and seamstress rolled their eyes to each other when she wasn't looking.

The mourning was brief—the reading of the will, and then the great expectation.

The combined time of waiting for Estella and "Vecchio Cavaliere" Swangarden's reluctance to step over the threshold into the afterlife has forced the Nazarene to remain neutral; he went about his business and was briefly entertained by Estella when she could get away. He grew fonder of her with each passing day, never admitting that the fantasy was self-deceiving.

As proud as he was of his vigor and youthful stature over old man Swangarden, old age snuck up on him swiftly; he was committed to performing only in those days and had to conclude, sadly, that legend is held up in the poverty of lost poetic themes. Time waiting has taken its toll. The shaving mirror has likened him to a bankrupt artwork that can no longer stand the test of time.

Nazareno sat on a folding chair by a great window that overlooked the avenue below his modest apartment. Dressed messily in a V-neck t-shirt and plaid pajama bottoms, he sat quietly sipping a beer, watching the traffic light change colors. A pale *eau de Nil* gentle green rounded off the curves and bumpers of sleek automobiles racing the light; hues changing every few seconds created warm amber circular bubbles that rolled heavily from the edge of a woman's umbrella, uniting thin streams of rain splashing willy-nilly around her shoes.

A quick hitch in the young lady's giddy-yap excited her motion to step lively across the intersection, advancing to safety on the other side.

Finally, red completed the cadence, bringing calm to the avenue and allowing for a brief moment of thought until the next race.

Over and over this sequence of trite, predictable visuals repeated; an idle arm sometimes hung from a rolled-down window, pinching a cigarette to near crumbling. An occasional cloud of smoke would puff from a twisted wing side glass. relieving the driver from sleepiness, reviving ventilation with a cool snap of stale old spice to conjure a daydream from an otherwise boring ride home from the office.

It was here that most commuters lived out the quiet desperation of their everyday lives; not in front of fireplaces and stylish living rooms with fern plants and puppy dogs portrayed in adverts, but behind the steering wheel of a Buick, Ford, or Chevy. The second home-on-wheels where a man could be himself and collect his thoughts before returning home to the deluxe little ranch-style home with a picket fence and garage, a steal at twelve percent interest over thirty years fixed—the aloneness of a Hopper painting.

The doting wife in the modern kitchen was most likely working a nine-to-five office job to help make ends meet—so much for the American dream. "Trade-in your jalopy for a pick-up truck in a few years; it will pay for itself," the man said.

Reno missed much of this—the domestic humdrum, the marital bliss, the housebreaking of the married man; discipline and routine, the gentlemanly arts—putting the toilette seat down after use and wiping the drips around the family commode.

He watched from the inside out. He never had a wife or children. Time passed much too quickly. Good health kept him from want and need of any real care from another, his genes were of good peasant stock.; always in flux with new amazement of how vast and ever-changing this new culture was... but even that once-never-ending wonderment was growing small to him lately. His days in Paris, Texas were over, and now, it's the city life with Estella—or so he thought.

The mysterious ocean was so vast; the world's ocean that carried him—a fugitive son who gambled on the sea of joy—to America. One with Odysseus to unchartered lands was something he felt he could pour into a bottle and watch for amusement as Poseidon had.

Is it possible that this "great clock" is a part of all of us?

Monte's timepiece that became Lydia;

Or she became it.

Miss Havisham's clock became Miss Havisham;

Or she became it.

Can we transfer the time on that clock through consciousness from person to person?

Even if the persons have never met?

Only to have ever existed to each other by each secret that the keeper holds?

Can each of us witness the gravity of a stranger's experience on the mere coincidence of a

The timeline they intersect with?

As Reno watched from his window, streets began to fill as noon rises.

The people on the street were becoming like seconds on that great clock again.

Each number following the next, with no attachment or fundamental connection at all.

Frozen. Separate from the science of time and unity.

Blank faces—no connection to the one face that passed before.

Oblivious to the one after.

Faces, arms, limbs... peddling forward; others counter against the flow like salmon moving forward also against the stream.

All directions lead onward.

Those who intentionally spin backward do not miss time; they miss opportunities.

Miss Havisham will never see the light of day because she stopped the clock.

Sufficient unto the moment is the appearance of reality.

Reno sees across the mass of people the young woman who worked at the Deli across the street, trotting along to deliver lunch to the florist on Dumont Ave. Her hair pulled back into a silk kerchief and her apron still tied daintily across her waist. She transforms into his beloved Mela. That spring morning in the fields by the storehouse.

"Carmella, I will find you, my little apple."

Snorts and snickers from behind a bush—the innocence of a shadow from behind an old screen door.

"Come out, Mela; don't be afraid, the future is not so bad. I am here, bringing youth and romance as my sword and shield. I will protect you. I will take you away; this meager home garden will become a kingdom. And you will become my bride and my queen. Do not fear the light, my little angel, I see it to… the long road and the darkness behind.

"Let me hold your hand? It is warm against my damp and clammy skin.

I am dying, my sweetheart.

However, I must tell you now before it is too late—now that you can hear me, now that you are near—beyond the threshold awaiting me, closer than I can ever remember you. How different you are now than in my memory… I must confess my memory is weak; much has changed over the years. In my dreams, you are bigger, brighter, more beautiful than life.

Now you are bigger than death."

I will not make it back home, Carmella. I promised I would see you once more, but things change."

The pain spread across Reno's chest; a dull ache caused numbness in his arm. His eyelids began to sag as if tiny sailors were dangling from his lashes, pulling the shades down.

In a consciousness that was brought on by an energy that was ancient and omnipresent, a whirlwind of whispers tickled his ears. Something was being forced or perceived from another place. It was an intrusion, to say the least; impossible to say who this figurine was being molded from dream dust, however extraordinary—something was happening. A new character bringing unsettled business was making its presence known, and it seems to have brought a friend. A horrible intrusion into a dying man's last dream—or maybe this is the way it is when life flashes before you as the song goes.

That's life,
As funny as it may seem,
Some people get their kicks,
Drop-in on a dream…
Hail Mary, full of grace, the Lord is with thee.
Pray for us sinners,
Now, at the hour of our death, Amen.
Faith grew in my mother's womb.
A baby I entered the door of Dharma
I studied the Buddha's teaching.
A man I lived alone in caves,
Though demons, ghosts, and devils multiply,
I am not afraid…
(And to quote the parlance of our times)
    In a gadda da Vida, honey
    Don't you know that I'm lovin' you
    In a gadda da Vida, baby
    Don't you know that I'll always be true
Oh, won't you come with me
And take my hand
Oh, won't you come with me
And walk this land
Please take my hand
In a gadda da Vida, honey
Don't you know that I'm lovin' you
In a gadda da Vida, baby
Don't you know that I'll always be true

Oh, won't you come with me
And take my hand
Oh, won't you come with me
And walk this land
Please take my hand…
The delirium flows; a raven crows.
An iron butterfly is pressed into vinyl.

It is possible, perhaps, that two people or a group might find each other in a sea of dimensional chaos—images and feelings that flow in life unnoticed but connect through a current of snaps and discharges. The reincarnation of unreleased or forgotten episodes… seconds, hours, hundreds of years.

"There, there! I know nothing of days of the week; I know nothing of the weeks of the year,"- expounds Miss Havisham. She has become my Mela now! No, not at all— is that you, Estella?"

She is well dressed and is wearing makeup, which could indicate either that she is on her way to or from work at a job where personal appearance is important, or that she is on her way to or from a social occasion.

She has removed only one glove, which may indicate either that she is distracted, that she is in a hurry and can stop only for a moment; or simply that she has just come in from outside and has not yet warmed up. But the latter possibility seems unlikely, for there is a small empty plate on the table, in front of her cup and saucer, suggesting that she may have eaten a snack and been sitting at this spot for some time.

And then, just like that, there was Monte—whom Reno has never known—and his friend was Lydia, leaping the turnstiles, racing the Spector. It was Lydia, the goddess Persephone, the duality of a woman on the threshold of youth, yearning for the freedom of maturity.

I never believed your premature death was convenient. She danced and leaped, never so graceful was such a giant. Those shoes…

she was wearing the shoes, my finest creation—an athletic sneaker, huge in length and width but feminine with style and poise and grace. the colors soft, finest leather, sparkles, and astral markings—Juliet's slippers. That night at the arena when she wore them for the first time... Atlantis Obscura—the gorgeous Amazon woman from New Jersey—full-blooded and beautiful; she wipes the blood of memory away and leaves Ithaca once more. The legendary quest—to become the finest one—is a delight that becomes all the more poignant.

And now, you have settled here—a pagan delight. The fame of your great virtue will never die. The immortal gods will lift a song for all humankind. A glorious song in praise of self-possessed Lydia.

> Oh, Lydia! Oh, Lydia! Say, have you met Lydia?
> Oh! Lydia, the tattooed lady
> When her muscles start relaxin'
> Up the hill comes Andrew Jackson
> Lydia, oh! Lydia, that "Encyclopedia"
> Oh! Lydia, the champ of them all

Please allow me to confess—Estella was no prize for me. I have gotten away with nothing. I am dying, and she is off. I am here alone—why are you jumping and playing, not listening? So unlike you—wait, you are dead—yes, I was at the cremation, yes, me and Este...

Who is that man with her? He is standing about like a Napoleon claiming victory and having never fought a battle. Odd little man; is he dead too? What business has he here? I am in purgatory—not Hades, I don't think. I do not know him. Does Lydia stop playing? What is going on? Who is this man? What does he want?"

A sudden shock came over me... Love letters! He has love letters! *Had*—poor soul what can we say about this Lydia? We are both the blame, guilty of his crime. I am being asked to carry your sins as well as his, Lydia—whoever he is, there is only one way to know. Your back Lydia... Am I to live out my purgatory in reprehensible madness? Please, help me to understand. I am alone. The shade turned about, revealing her back and broadside, carefully removing the shawl from across her shoulders.

"She is clean!"

The whole of the back is restored, no trace of the grotesque procedure—only smooth pale white skin, more silken than I remember it. Her hair so brown and fallen, so different than remember, so changed, so normal in size. Is it Lydia? What trick is this?

Who is this pale creature, so much the same and yet so different, with smirks and giggles, cannot speak a word—so horrible? I feel clammy, chillness emanating from her. Never a living thing—never! She has done away with Lydia completely.

Are the dark angel swings low, as he might certainly weave dreams unto Nazareno "Reno" Papilla: the Nazarene, the breast of life who has become a dying hotel for rebel souls and unfulfilled miscreants of all kinds to settle into and haunt while waiting for their number to come up?

Lydia is gone, this fiend before me has swallowed her in death. There are strangers above me, below me, and all around me; each one twists with electricity, the current of eternity. Who is Monte? I hear that name... I do not know him.

It is quite possible Monte is contemplating death or has already succeeded in taking his own life. If he is—or was, or might have been—connected to Lydia or the other, then I suppose getting caught in cross-transmission would explain how he is in paradise lost. One foot on earth, one foot in this nightmare. I, Reno Papilla, hover above the living, looking for Mela, my little apple... I promised I would come back. I promised.

Estella, I suppose will find out about me, my passing; Xi will be over with the won ton soup only to find me at room temperature...

The End.